Trail's End

A Collection of Western Short Stories

A Zimbell House Anthology

Trail's End

A Collection of Western Short Stories

A Zimbell House Anthology

ZIMBELL HOUSE
PUBLISHING
UNION LAKE, MICHIGAN

For permission requests, write to the publisher:
"Attention: Permissions Coordinator"
Zimbell House Publishing
PO Box 1172
Union Lake, Michigan 48387
mail to: info@zimbellhousepublishing.com

© 2018 Zimbell House Publishing et al.

Published in the United States by Zimbell House Publishing
http://www.ZimbellHousePublishing.com
All Rights Reserved

Trade Paper ISBN: 978-1-947210-52-3
Kindle ISBN: 978-1-947210-53-0
Digital ISBN: 978-1-947210-54-7
Library of Congress Control Number: 2018906583

First Edition: June/2018
10 9 8 7 6 5 4 3 2 1

ZIMBELL HOUSE PUBLISHING
UNION LAKE

Acknowledgments

Zimbell House Publishing would like to thank all those that contributed to this anthology. We chose to showcase eight new voices that best represented our vision for this work.

We would also like to thank our Zimbell House team for all their hard work and dedication to these projects.

Contents

Blue Flower Woman

Steve Carr

Flora sat on the bench outside the dry goods store. She watched the wagons loaded with lumber and barrels being pulled through the muddy street by teams of horses and mules. Her patchwork gingham dress fit her nicely, but she tugged at it and squirmed about as if she were trapped in the dress.

I stood nearby, leaning against the rail on the wooden walkway in front of the store, saloon, and barbershop. It was taking some getting used to that an actual town was springing up this far west. Being on an ocean shipping route made that possible.

I looked eastward and then looked at Flora and said, "Are you okay?"

She put her fingers on the red bandana around her neck and nodded.

The wagon leaned to the left, its rear left wheel broken nearly in half was lying in the dirt a few feet away. Joshua Bigelow was sitting in the tall bright green prairie grass watching a grasshopper crawl across the back of his hand.

"I'll say it again, now what?" he said.

I looked westward, across the prairie that stretched all the way to the horizon. "It's not my fault that we've lost two wheels in less than a hundred miles."

"Buy the two-hundred-dollar wagon and not the four-hundred-dollar one," Joshua said, doing an uncanny impression of my voice. The grasshopper jumped from his hand. "I told you when we bought it that the wheels wouldn't last. It's not as if we couldn't have afforded a better wagon."

I kicked at the ground with the tip of my boot, sending up a small cloud of dirt, and looked up at the white sun that seemed to fill the entire sky. I pushed my hat back on my head and wiped sweat from my forehead with the back of my hand. A hawk circling above us let out a loud screech and dived toward the earth, momentarily disappeared in the tall grass and then ascended with a field mouse in its talons. As it flew off, I said, "We've got the mules."

Joshua looked at me as if I was crazy. "We're going to pack the rifles, flour, lard, beans, apples, bacon, coffee and salt, along with the pots and pans, water kegs, tools, clothes, sleeping rolls and animal hides along with the money on the back of six mules and ride on them all the way to Oregon?"

I hated to admit when Joshua was right. "Not everything," I said. "We'll take the money and just whatever supplies we'll absolutely need."

He straightened the bright red bandana tied around his neck. "What we need is to get across these plains without having our scalps detached from our heads," he said.

I could feel the hairs raise on the back of my neck. "Maybe we should have hooked up with a wagon train instead of going it alone," I said.

"We couldn't chance being recognized by anyone who might be coming from Chicago," he said. "Our faces are probably posted all over the city."

At that moment Joshua jumped up and pointed eastward. "Look," he shouted.

At a great distance, but discernible, was a wagon heading in our direction. Sunlight made its white canvas cover gleam amidst the surrounding prairie grass.

I pulled my gun from the holster and checked the cylinder. There were five bullets. I put the gun back in the holster. "How far away do you think it is?" I said.

Joshua climbed up onto the seat of the wagon. "It's hard to tell. Maybe a half hour away." From the seat, he pulled a rifle out of the inside of the wagon.

I took the lid off the water barrel attached to the side of the wagon and removed my hat. Using the tin dipper, I scooped out some water and poured it over my head and into my mouth. It was warm almost to the point of being hot yet refreshing. With water dripping from my hair and face, I put the lid and dipper back, put my hat back on and walked to the rear of the wagon. Joshua was sitting on the barrel of apples in the back of the wagon bed with a rifle across his lap.

He bit into an apple that crunched between his teeth. As he chewed it, he said, "You shouldn't be wasting water."

"We can't take it all with us on the mules anyway," I said.

"Maybe these folks coming this way might have an extra wheel they'd give us."

I turned and saw the wagon was closer and that two men were sitting on the front seat, one was handling the reins on the team of mules pulling the wagon. "Why would they give away a wheel even if they had an extra?"

He threw the apple core into the grass and said, "Didn't I say maybe? For someone with an education, you sure don't listen very well."

I leaned back against the wagon and watched a small herd of buffalo running across the prairie in the distance. Though not many in number, they kicked up a thick cloud of dirt that hung in the air above them. "I wonder what they're running from?"

Joshua leaned out of the wagon, looked at the buffalo, and then sat back. "As long as it's not a Sioux war party on horseback, I don't really care."

My attention was drawn back to the approaching wagon when one of the two men lifted his hat in the air and shouted, "Howdy, strangers."

I removed my hat and waved it. "Howdy."

Joshua and I said nothing to each other as the wagon drew closer and then came to a stop about ten yards behind us. One of the men jumped down from the wagon. He was tall, bulky and had a scraggly red beard that hung to the middle of his chest. He kept his hand on the handle of his gun sticking out of his holster.

"Looks like you've had a bit of misfortune," he said with a thick Irish accent and nodding toward the broken wheel.

"We lose wheels the same way some people lose their rotten teeth," I said. "They just break up and fall off and cause a whole lot of grief."

He let out a guffaw. "This ain't a good place to be alone and lose your wheels or your teeth," he said. "My name's Pat O'Shea." He pointed to the other man seated on the wagon. "That's my brother, Ryan."

Ryan was smaller in build and had a handlebar mustache. He appeared younger than Pat. He had a scowl on his face. There were bright red scratch marks across his left cheek.

"I'm Robert Langford, and this is Joshua Bigelow," I said, waving my hand toward Joshua who had shifted the rifle and had the barrel pointing out of the wagon.

"We're originally from Dublin," Pat said. "We lived in Chicago for a couple of years but couldn't make a go of it, so we're going west like everyone else. We plan on settling in Oregon and take up farming. Where are you headed?"

"California," Joshua said loudly before I could answer. "We're coming from Kansas City."

Pat's eyes narrowed, and he looked at Joshua and then back at me. "Seems you'd be taking a more southern route."

"We wanted to see what some of the northern territories was like. We're turning south when we reach the settlement at Rapid Creek," Joshua said.

"That's where we're headed," Pat said. "It's about four to five days ride from here."

"That's what we figured," Joshua said.

At that moment a woman cried out from inside their wagon. "K-'tay nee 'ay. K-'tay nee 'ay," she repeated.

"Who's that?" I said.

"Some squaw we found taking a bath in a stream a couple days back," he said. "She's feisty and likes to bite and scratch." He held out his arm, showing the imprint of teeth marks on his skin that was inflamed around the bite.

"What are you doing with her?" Joshua said.

Pat's smile was lecherous. "What you do with any woman," he said. "We'll let her go when we get near the settlement."

"Speaking of the settlement, do you have a wheel we can borrow until we get there to get a new one?" I said.

He lifted his hat, scratched his head, and said, "Hold on." He walked over to his wagon and had a whispered conversation with Ryan. He returned and said, "We'll lend you a wheel for twenty dollars, but we don't plan to continue on until the morning."

I glanced at Joshua who nodded.

"It's a deal," I said.

Before turning to go back to his wagon, he stared intently at my face, and then Joshua's. "I have this funny feeling I've seen you two somewhere before."

When Pat was out of earshot, Joshua said, "Those two are trouble."

The howl of coyotes reverberated in the night. A luminous crescent moon cast a dim light across the prairie. To the south, rock formations with short, jagged peaks jutted up from the landscape. A steady hot breeze made the grass bend back and forth, forming ocean-like currents. The campfire that the two brothers had built burned brightly and sent glowing red embers and ash up into the sky.

The Sioux woman was sitting on the ground, her wrists tied to a wheel of their wagon. Her buckskin dress was torn below her left breast, and her hair was disheveled. There was a bruise on her right cheek, and her lower lip was swollen. Her moccasins were on the ground next to her. I couldn't tell her exact age, but she appeared to be in her twenties.

I sat on a mound of dirt near the fire.

Pat and Ryan were asleep in their wagon. Their loud snoring filtered through the canvas cover. Earlier I had watched Joshua take a dipper of water to the woman. Mistrustful and skittish, it took several minutes before he was able to convince her to drink the water. When she finally did she quickly gulped it down. He then fed her some beans and hardtack by hand. He sat with her for the next couple of hours, neither of them saying anything. Before walking away from her and joining me at the fire, he laid a blanket across her legs.

"We have to set her free," he said, whispering.

"Then what?" I said. "Those two might try to kill her and us. And if she got to her tribe before we get to the settlement, then we'll have every Sioux in this territory on our tails and looking to do a lot worse to us than Pat and Ryan are doing to her."

"I never took you to be such a coward," he said. He untied his red bandana, took it from his neck and shook it out, and then put it back on.

I knew he was right. I didn't like at all the choice of either being shot by Pat or Ryan or skinned alive by the Indians. "I'll put out the fire, and then you cut her free," I said.

While he got a knife from the wagon, I threw dirt on the fire. Through the haze of smoke from the extinguished flames, I watched him cut the rope around her wrists.

Instantly she grabbed the knife from his hand and jumped on him, and pinned him to the ground. She held the edge of the knife blade to his neck. She placed her free hand across his mouth and shook her head and then slowly stood up.

Neither Joshua nor I moved or said a word as she climbed into their wagon. There was only the slightest sound of a struggle. The snoring ceased. She jumped out of the wagon with the knife dripping blood. She walked over to Joshua who was sitting up and handed him the knife and then put on her moccasins.

She pulled a pale blue crocus from the ground, rubbed her fingers on the petal and then pointed to Joshua's blue eyes and patted her chest. "Toh vah koh'-peevvash-tem'-in- nah wee'-ahn," she said. She then pointed at Joshua.

"Joshua," he said haltingly.

She then pointed at me.

"Robert," Joshua said.

She patted the spare wheel hooked onto the side of their wagon and then pointed at our wagon.

As Joshua and I put their wheel on our wagon, she pushed aside some of the dirt from the fire and dug out a still smoldering ember. She fanned it with her hand and blew on it until a flame erupted and then built a small fire. She climbed into their wagon and came out a few minutes later with a straw broom and a poster.

She handed the poster to me and pointed at us.

On one side the poster was a hand-drawn map of part of Chicago and on the other side printed in black ink were sketches of Joshua and me. Above our faces were the words, "Wanted for bank robbery. $2,000 reward for their capture and the return of the money." At the bottom of the paper was the Chicago bank's name and address and the name of the bank president.

When the wheel was on, and their mules were hooked up to ours, she stuck the straw end of the broom in the fire, and with it fully ablaze she then tossed it into the wagon.

I tossed the wanted poster in after it.

As the hazy yellow light of dawn spread across the morning sky, we began to ride westward. Behind us, the other wagon was engulfed in flames.

Blue Flower Woman followed us on foot.

Rapid Creek was a swift-moving, narrow creek that wound its way through verdant low-lying woods and meadows before entering the pine-covered mountains of the Black Hills. The settlement that had been established along the creek's banks consisted of about twenty log cabin-like structures and some sod houses. A small Army garrison was stationed there to protect the settlement from the Sioux, but the soldiers spent most of their time in the two saloons swilling whiskey with the prospectors taking a break from searching for gold in the nearby western hills.

We parked the wagon alongside the creek just outside the settlement. In the time it had taken to get from where we left the burning O'Shea wagon to the settlement, Joshua and Blue Flower Woman had taught each other enough of each other's language, along with speaking with their hands, to communicate with each other.

Our second night there he told her to stay in the wagon.

She didn't like being told what to do and reacted as always by crossing her arms and glaring at him. As we began to leave she sat down at the back opening of the wagon and in the glow of moonlight she combed her long black hair with a comb Joshua had given her.

"She's attached herself to us, and you're not helping any," I said to him as we walked along the muddy path going into the settlement.

"After what the O'Sheas did to her, going back to her people might get her killed or get a lot of settlers killed," he said.

"Having a Sioux woman with us might get us killed," I said.

We stopped outside a door with a board next to it with the word 'saloon' painted on it. The cacophonous noise from inside echoed out. We kicked the mud from our boots and opened the door. A wave of noxious smells greeted us; body odors, vomit, wet earth, whiskey. The saloon was dimly lit by oil lamps affixed to the walls. In one corner four soldiers sat around a table playing cards. At two other tables, prospectors most likely given their nearly ragged and unkempt appearances, noisily argued as they drank whiskey from small glasses. In the middle of the room, two shirtless men wrestled on the floor. A dozen men encircled them, yelling and making bets.

A line of men stood shoulder to shoulder along the bar. Two bartenders were behind the bar, rapidly refilling the glasses of whiskey. Other than the soldiers, we were the only men wearing holsters and guns.

As we walked to the bar, I tried to ignore the inquisitive stares we were getting. We had washed our clothes, bathed and shaved in the creek, so along with being strangers, we were the only two clean men in the place. At the bar, we squeezed in between two foul-smelling men with scraggly beards.

"Two whiskeys," Joshua called out and rapped his knuckles on the bar.

Carrying a bottle of whiskey, the bartender picked up two glasses and walked over to us. He placed the glasses on the bar and looked us over. "You're new here," he said. "You planning on prospecting for gold?"

"No, just passing through on the way west," I said.

He poured whiskey into the glasses. "You with a train?"

"No, by ourselves," I said. "Our wagon is down by the creek."

Joshua picked up his glass, took a sip and coughed harshly. "This stuff is awful."

"It's the best we got," the bartender said.

I took a sip of my whiskey and nearly spit it out as it burned my throat.

"You're taking chances leaving your wagon untended if it's just you two," he said. "Thieves will strip a wagon clean of anything valuable if they get a chance. Some of the prospectors are pretty desperate."

Joshua and I put our glasses on the bar at the same time. I threw the coins for the whiskey on the bar and then we turned and rushed out of the saloon. We ran through the mud all the way to the wagon. Our bedrolls, clothes, some of our tools, and an overturned barrel of flour was lying on the ground around the wagon.

Joshua climbed into the wagon, and then stuck his head out. "She's not here, and they've taken practically everything, including our box of bullets."

"What about the money?"

I watched from outside the wagon as he searched among the small pile of things left behind by the thieves. "It's gone," he said climbing out of the wagon.

"They must have taken Blue Flower Woman with them," I said.

"She'll be killed—"

"Joshua ... Robert," Blue Flower Woman said as she stepped out of the darkness of the nearby trees. She had the bank bag containing the money in her arms.

Joshua ran to her. "Are you okay?"

She nodded. "Men come. See me. I run. Hide," she said. She handed him the bag. "Mah-zah'-skah. Money."

"How did she know?" I said.

"It doesn't matter," Joshua said. "We need to get out of here now before anyone comes back looking for her or to take what little we have left."

By dawn, we continued our trek westward, across the great northern plains.

We arrived at the mountain pass at the same time as winter. Unable to pull us any further in the deep snow, we unhooked the mules from the wagon but kept them tied up at nearby trees. We knew that a band of Paiute Indians had been following us but didn't hear them the night they stole the mules.

The little amount of food supplies we had managed to buy from other travelers and small encampments along the way ran out soon after that. I shot the last bullet we had at a deer but missed.

Joshua came down with a fever and lay sweating, shivering and delirious under a buffalo hide we had bought from a soldier who had deserted and was traveling alone to California. Blue Flower Woman slept under the hide with Joshua during the night, warming him with her body heat and wiping the sweat from his face with his red bandana.

During the nights I stayed outside, keeping the campfire going, using tree branches and twigs and whatever boards could be ripped from the wagon without exposing the inside to the weather. I fed the fire fistfuls of the money to keep it ablaze until most of the money had been burned, and then I tossed in the bank bag.

Maybe it was the fire that kept the wolves at bay, but I heard them as they encircled our encampment and their frequent howls pierced the darkness beyond the trees.

During the days Blue Flower Woman would disappear into the woods, taking with her our only knife, and return carrying a slain rabbit, raccoon or a handful of birds that I skinned or plucked and cooked on a spit over the fire. She tried to feed Joshua some of the cooked meat by hand, but he ate very little.

A night when Joshua had taken a turn for the worse, and lay unconscious, his breathing labored, the wolves attacked.

First one, then another, then two more, crept out of the woods, their teeth bared, the hair on their backs raised. They were surrounding me. I pulled a branch from the fire and swung the fire-tipped tree limb at them as they growled viciously.

Blue Flower Woman jumped out of the wagon with the knife grasped in her hand. She attacked the nearest wolf, plunging the knife into its skull as it leapt at her. She pulled the knife from the wolf's head, tilted her head back, opened her mouth wide and let out a high-pitched screech. The wolves ran back into the woods, and she followed them.

I watched and waited for her return but felt certain the wolves had gotten her.

Two mornings later, Joshua died.

That afternoon, Blue Flower Woman emerged from the woods followed by four soldiers on horseback.

"Bring help," she said, pointing to the soldiers. "Joshua?"

"He's gone," I told her.

She climbed into the wagon. A few moments later I heard her mournfully chanting in Lakota.

California Trail

Joanna Blair

DAILY EVENING GAZETTE January 5, 1856

NEEDED: Strong woman, must cook, good with children, drive a team, to accompany widower and children on the trail to California. Your own homestead is payment. Contact Edward Persons, Independence Missouri.

January 7, 1856

Dear Edward,

My name is Cora. I saw your advert in the paper for help on the California trail. I am a strong woman, used to working hard. I grew up on a farm. I currently help my sister with her two young children. How many children do you have? I am interested in accompanying you.

Sincerely,
Cora Masterson

Edward,

I will see you the last Saturday in January. Thank you for the address. Ages seven, five, and three are all wonderful ages, though I do understand why your housekeeper would want to stay with family and not travel with you.

I look forward to meeting them and discussing details if we both think this is a good fit.

Cora

March 29, 1856

Dear Lillian,

Well, here I am three days into our journey. You'll be happy to hear I'm well taken care of despite the fact I'm in charge of three rambunctious children. We walk alongside the wagon until the children tire. Little Eddy tires fastest, but of course will never admit it. Clara, at five, loves to run ahead which proves frustrating, but otherwise, she is a pleasant child who will sit playing with her rag doll for hours if allowed. Elora, the seven-year-old, is a little mother. I suppose it comes naturally when you lose yours, you would know better than me since I was little like Eddy when mama died. I feel I can relate to the children because we all lost our mother at a young age. Edward did not, but left his mother in Boston years ago.

He keeps the oxen, along with his milk cow, and takes turns with me keeping guard, though there haven't been any dangers yet—aside from the chill at night.

Did you get snow on the twenty-second? We had some overnight, though by the time we breakfasted it had mostly melted.

Edward is friendly to me, quite chatty for a man, so it passes the time. I know a lot about him, and I suppose he knows an awful lot about me now. Imagine how well we'll know the entire group by the time we reach California?

There's been some talk amongst other women saying it's inappropriate I'm traveling with him, but how else would he bring his children along? A sixty-year-old woman, settled in her ways would have been more appropriate they say, but she would have a much harder time on the trail.

I sleep in the wagon with the children, and he sleeps outside under the wagon. Nothing inappropriate, but women anywhere have to find something to gossip about don't they? There are twenty-three women, about thirty men, and thirty or so children. A couple women are snubbing me, but I enjoy the company of Mrs. Meer's oldest daughter, Liza, who is nineteen, like me, but married with a baby. They are so brave for coming on the journey, but when you have the choice of starving to death at home or accompany the family to a better life. You choose hope.

I am well, so try not to worry about me,

Your sister,

Cora

April 15

Dear Lillian,

Last night was the scariest of all the nights so far. The wagons were circled up for the night, and everyone had gone to sleep when the howling began. Normally it wouldn't concern me, but knowing Edward and others were sleeping right outside, I became panicked. It seems the wolves were after scraps of food left behind. Edward and most of the men sleep with their rifles so I peeked out the wagon and could see them standing there waiting to see what the wolves chose to do. The moon was almost full, the sky clear, I almost expected Indians to ride in after them, but alas I have not seen any yet. In the moonlight, I could see the wolves coming closer and closer as if searching for food. They picked at pieces of something, probably bread children had dropped while eating, but they didn't try to attack anyone, so we all waited. I'm pretty sure all the adults were awake, watching at this point. I could feel my heart pounding in my head.

Little Eddy and Clara slept through the howling, bless their souls, but Elora woke and clung to me, so I sat back inside the wagon, listening to the nearness of the wolves and stillness of the night. Finally.

I was told the next morning one wolf got too brave and almost climbed into Mr. Magnan's tent, so he shot the wolf, so some other men shot as well, and scared the rest off. Wolf meat isn't the tastiest, but they'll have the fur to trade at our next big stop in Fort Kearney.

I'm not sure I should send you this because I don't want you worrying about me. However, I thought it rather exciting in comparison to the other details of my life on the trail. Walking, walking, more walking, starting fires, cooking. It's pleasant. I like having others to talk with all the time. I also enjoy the hard work, and I'm sleeping better than I ever have. Edward says it's all the sunshine and outside air. Makes you sleep better.

The children have been really well behaved. They're growing so accustomed to me already I'm going to have a really hard time leaving them for my own homestead when we arrive, but I am trying not to think of it and just be happy in the present with them. Speaking of which, I can hear Elora and Clara bickering about something, so I suppose I should see what is going on. They truly are good children though.

Your brave sister,

Cora

May 14, 1856

Dear Lillian,

Thank you for your note! It was waiting for me at Fort Kearney! Now I can't wait to see if others you write arrive before I do. Isn't the postal system amazing? You will receive all my letters together, but here is my latest update.

Would you believe they are charging at least five times what we paid in Missouri for pork and beans? Soap, tools, anything you might need on the trail has been jacked up considerably, and people pay the price because this is the only place for miles around to buy supplies. Thankfully we packed enough dried goods I didn't need anything, but Edward needed a part for the wagon wheel. He was not too pleased with the price. I wonder how expensive things will be in California.

We arrived late last night. I'm glad Jubal will think me to be in Maine if he asks. He is extremely clever so please be diligent and tell anyone else who asks that's where I've gone.

We are all very careful on the trail, and I'm sure by California I'll be so strong and wise, able to deflect any man who tries to harm me. I have wit and brawn, so do not fret. It will only make you ill, and I'd hate for my only sister to be ill while I am having a splendid time on the trail.

I'm safe and also do not worry about me and who I marry. I will marry for love one day.

Speaking of love, little Eddy has me wrapped around his finger. Today one of the cats the Magnans brought had kittens and when he asked if we could have one I couldn't resist his big blue pleading eyes. The kittens have to stay in the wagon for some time, and even then there's risk of it running off, but in a few weeks, we'll have a kitten added to our wagon. Big Ed, as I've come to call him, doesn't know any of this yet, but I don't think he will mind. He's a huge man, eats a lot, but has a soft heart. It's endearing to observe him singing or playing with his children in the evening. I often set back and find myself intruding on their family moments, but they never treat me like an intruder. I'm feeling very much part of their family.

The entire wagon train feels very much like a family, and since you were really the only family I knew, I am learning the comfort and safety one feels within a family. But you will always be my true family.

I will look for a letter from you at the next fort. Fort Laramie. Seems so far away, but time is flying.

I'll be in California before I know it.

Love your only sister,

Cora

June 8, 1856

Dear Lillian,

I know in my last letter I said time was flying, however now I must disagree. It is dragging like the oxen pulling our wagons.

Remember the ocean in Maine? How you could look out and see nothing but blue-grey as far as the eye could see. The prairie is like that except all I see is grass. Yellow and brown waves of tall grass billowing in the breeze. Picture hayfields instead of the ocean, as far as the eye can see, day after day. There's so much space and openness I try not to dwell on it, or it overwhelms me. I much prefer having some trees around to enclose the space.

I don't mean to depress you, I AM fine. I'm just annoyed with Mrs. Pritchard and her holier than thou attitude. She constantly gives me looks. Then last evening while we were finishing supper she walked away and said she didn't understand why we didn't get married since we were acting like we were already. Simply because we sat on a blanket next to each other? Why can't I sit and chat with Big Ed while we eat? The children do the majority of talking anyhow. I told her we weren't doing anything like married people do and she accused us of walking off one night unchaperoned. Which maybe we did, while the children were asleep. It was a beautiful evening.

Too nice to sleep. She's so nosy and has nothing else better to do with her time than judge others.

Tonight, I have every intention of making sure she sees how chaste I am. Or on the other hand, I may just kiss Big Ed right in front of her because that would really give her something to talk about. And no, he has not kissed me. Though I think he almost wanted to the other evening.

He's too much of a gentleman, and we haven't discussed the future. I think I may tell him about Jubal though, in case he does discover my whereabouts. I think he would protect me. I feel safe most nights. Our wagons camp in a circle, so if for some reason anything were to happen help is all around me. Of course, when we were at the fort with soldiers plodding around all hours of the night, I felt even safer. I feel confident our guide, and the other men know how to handle anything thrown our way.

Don't worry about me,

Cora

June 21, 1856

Dearest Lillian,

We reached the crossing on the Platte River finally! The river is bigger than I expected. I'd guess it to be a hundred yards across. It's still deep, about ten feet, from the spring rain we've been having so we ferried across yesterday. The animals were able to swim because for a river it is rather shallow. Five dollars for a wagon to cross the river! There was a bridge built, but soldiers dismantled it this past winter. Rumor has it they're building a new one, but for now, the only way across is the ferry or boat. The ferry is much safer than it used to be, with a pulley system that ensures we'll get across.

The water is stronger than any river I've seen. The undertow reminded me of the river in Orono.

Remember when we were children and father was still alive and we were on the bank of the river not far from the bridge, but I slipped and fell? The current pulled me under, but father grabbed me. We almost had a similar incident. When it's warmer, I'm going to make sure the children learn to swim. It could save their lives.

We were floating, the wagon on the ferry, and unbeknownst to us, little Eddy had wandered away from the group of us standing patiently waiting. The child is three and refuses to be held any longer. Apparently, he grew curious, looking for fish in the river, and wandered too close to the edge of the ferry. We hit a small wave, and the child lost his footing and tumbled headfirst into the river. Thankfully Big Ed stood nearby and moved faster than a horse spooked by lightning grabbing hold of his leg. So, Eddy was barely in the water, but everyone got shook up. He clung to me the rest of the crossing, which took about five minutes, and then he wouldn't let go all day.

We're blessed the crossing is much easier than it was ten years ago. We're all thankful to have survived. Thus far the only loss our party has suffered is poor Mrs. Bassett, the journey was just too much for her older body. She caught a chill and never recovered. Is it bad of me to say I don't miss her snide remarks about my inappropriate position? Well, I don't. She was friends with Mrs. Pritchard. Everyone is getting used to our arrangement. Even the children. I don't know how I will ever be able to leave the children.

I'm considering claiming land next to theirs so Ed can help me farm, and I can still take care of the children.

I hope you are well and enjoying the summer flowers. Are the roses blossoming yet? We still mostly see grass, so the river has been a beautiful change of scenery. We're camping along the banks tonight as I write and tomorrow we'll be on our way. I'll leave my letter at the trading post here.

Your sister,
Cora

July 1, 1856

Dear Lillian,

We passed Chimney Rock. It's a sight for sore eyes, sticking up in the middle of the prairie, giving you something else to look at. I'm noticing subtle changes in the way the grass is blowing. The sky is massive, so I spend a lot of time walking alongside the wagon looking at the clouds. The children enjoy finding rabbits or cows or angels in the shapes. My favorite, the other day Eddy said the cloud looked like a buffalo chasing a wagon. Only a child living out of a wagon for months on the prairie would come up with a comment like that.

Oh, I wanted to ask you. Have you seen Jubal around town? Please say you have. One of the men sited horse's hoof prints not far from our camp when they were on watch. They weren't any of our tracks. He thinks perhaps they belong to Indians, but Indians don't leave tracks. I need you to reassure me there is no way on God's green earth Jubal could have caught up with us. I am on guard now mentally expecting him to appear out of the tall grass. Tell me it is impossible.

Ed sensed something was wrong the other night after the sighting, so I broke down and told him everything about Jubal. I began with how he tricked us into believing father owed him money, to how I felt so indebted I fell for every lie and believed I was obligated to marry him. How I truly thought I loved him and how he grew obsessed with marrying me despite being twenty years my senior. Ed grew angrier by the second in his expressions as he listened, but he didn't say a word. He didn't accuse me of being gullible or too trustworthy. Then I told him how I snuck back father's rifle and mama's ring. They're not worth anything to him, so I can't imagine he will notice they're gone. I know I shouldn't have done that, but I suppose the fact I was leaving for good got to me and I figured I'd never see those things if I didn't take them back.

Ed doesn't think he'll notice and believes I made the right choice getting as far away from that man as possible. I hope he leaves you alone now I'm gone, he does after all still have money from us. He never did bother you though, for some reason he thought he'd get a large inheritance by marrying me, even though he'd already taken our money. You were smart to never fall for his cunning lies.

So, I hope and pray it is just Indians or outlaws on our trail. Isn't that funny? I want to see Indians. They're harmless, usually wanting to trade things, but they still intimidate the children. Elora screamed the first time she saw one. We sometimes find remnants of them stealing from graves, but they have not stolen from us living folks. We are quite safe I can assure you.

Your sister,
Cora

July 2, 1856

Dear Lillian,

Your letter reached Fort Laramie before me. I can believe Jubal is looking for me, and am thoroughly convinced it's his tracks we saw. I do wish he'd believed you when you told him I'd gone back to Maine. Figures he heard from someone—but wouldn't say who—that I'd gone west. I'm wondering if he bribed the postman.

What do you think he intends to do? He has nothing better to do with his time, so he is truly trailing behind us? Unbelievable. He's about two weeks late, but since he's alone, a stupid man traveling alone, I hope he dies on the trail. I am most certainly on guard. I do not think he will harm me since he still seems determined to marry me, but he's unpredictable.

You have not failed me as a big sister. I will be safe.

Cora

July 23, 1856

Dear Lillian,

We passed a Sioux village after Fort Laramie, so our guide and even Edward think it was simply Indians we saw. I am not convinced, especially after receiving your letter about Jubal once we reached Fort Laramie. They're so careful about making sure we can't see them. If they were Indians, they would want to trade with us. Indians happen upon us almost daily now looking for something to trade, and often someone in the wagon train needs to. I lay awake some nights praying it's not Jubal we hear. It's so scary out here alone knowing he could be catching up to us, but I am confident the men in our wagon train can handle anything that comes their way whether it be Indians or Jubal.

We've reached some pretty barren land. We were warned, but oh my is it hot in the blazing sun. Our skin, even with hats and bonnets will soon be leather and dark as the Indians. In this heat I keep the kids going by seeing who can collect the most buffalo chips. We gather them in bags during the day to burn at night with sagebrush since there aren't any other things growing. It's too hot to write any more.

Your sister,

Cora

August 4, 1856

Dear Lillian,

Today Mr. Mangan got bit by a rattlesnake. They were able to get the remedy into him to try and stop the poison from spreading, but they ended up having to cut off a limb. He is one of the more lighthearted men in the party and doesn't seem as upset about it as some of the other men would have been. Still, his wife now has to drive the team while he rests in the wagon. We are all going to be extra careful now.

Another family had dysentery, and two of them did not survive. It seems our wagon train is not exempt from hardships.

I check the tents every morning for lizards after one jumped out at me the other morning. I know they are harmless, but I still startled like a horse being spooked by a snake.

More startling was the buffalo herd that came pounding past us when we were closer to Laramie. Did I mention that? A black cloud swirled in our direction, almost like a threatening storm, moving with snorts, noses down, tails up, disregard for anything in their path. They stampeded right past and over-turned a wagon in their line of advance. Several people were hurt, but no one died. Two buffalo were shot, and I finally got to taste buffalo. It's surprisingly tender with a nice flavor. We dried strips left over and have had jerky for days in the desert, like today, when we can't find enough food.

Many in our party have taken to complaining and grumbling, I suppose it gives them something to talk about, but we all know it's hot. I would like for people to stop complaining. I find joy to counterbalance the complaints by watching the children's amazement at things. It keeps my spirits up when Eddy is thrilled about a small flower blooming in the desert. Each prickly pear cactus he points out. The fruit is not quite ripe according to our guide, or we would use gloves to pick them.

I believe we have another week or so in the desert and then we will near the Rocky Mountains. We're all looking forward to a reprieve from the sun. Is it hot in Missouri right now? How are you faring? How is the laundry business?

Your sister,

Cora

September 8, 1856

Dear Lillian,

I have been rather busy lately believe it or not. The sun from the desert made us so tired, but now we've reached the mountains rising up from the hot desert. Their steep trails are even more exhausting than the desert. The mountains gave way to more vegetation, though the roads, true to their name, are very rocky.

To keep the wagons from pressing on the animals the men have tied ropes to trees and the wagons and slowly lower them. This takes twice as long to travel, but it's much safer.

Our guide came around suggesting ways to lighten the wagon. We had to leave Ed's mother's hutch behind with a table. The table he said he could replace easily, but the hutch he brooded about. I left behind a few books that will do me no good in California. I kept the primer for Elora to use. She loves learning, and I try to tell her things from my memory. I hope there will be a school for her in California.

There are trees again which made us so thankful for some shade after days of the bare desert. I much prefer trees and am happy to hear the area surrounding San Francisco will have them.

We sit around the campfire in the evening, the days already growing shorter. Children run around, Mr. Potter plays his harmonica, and others join in song. I often sit with the women, and we share stories of home or trade recipes. Any new way to prepare biscuits and beans is a welcome treat. Our barrel of apples is almost empty. Flour and sugar are running low as well. Ed says we will be fine until we reach the Great Salt Lake.

I noticed this evening how muscular and lean he's gotten then realized you probably wouldn't recognize me with my darker skin and strong arms. I suppose this journey is changing us all.

We have not had any more suspicious footprints or sounds lately. Just squirrels, rabbits, and more Indians.

Your sister,

Cora

September 23, 1856

Dear Lillian,

We reached Salt Lake City. The mountains behind us were the most treacherous part of the trip. We're down two wagons and a few animals since the desert. But we've arrived.

The lake glistens below the surrounding mountains. Sparkling, it reminds me of Maine, if I close my eyes, partially letting just a glimpse of the lake, and breathe the air. I love water so much, it's the closest to the ocean I've felt since I left Maine.

We had a big celebration on the shore of the lake. Camping and eating food we'd just bought. Highway robbery for flour, thirteen dollars! I'm told California is even more expensive.

We danced long into the night as we're spending an extra day here to repair wagons, do laundry, and get situated for the last leg of our journey. There's so much hope felt tonight.

Cora

September 24, 1856

Lillian,

I'm writing just a day later because so much happened in just one day. Edward was repairing the wagon axle, and I was doing the dishes from breakfast when I heard a shout, "Cora!"

I turned my head, and I'm sure you guessed it already. Jubal. Can you believe he followed us out here? The mountains slowed us down, and he caught up. He claims he was always close behind just waiting for the right moment.

Well, he's too late. Even those who don't care much for me do NOT want anything bad to happen to me. Edward stood right up, an entire head taller than Jubal, and stared him down asking, "Who are you?"

"This lady's intended," Jubal said.

"Well that's not true because I'm her husband," Edward said. To which Jubal's face fumed red with anger.

He kicked over the dishpan and looked at me, "Is that true?"

I shrugged, and some of the others from our party circled around him. A couple men even pulled out rifles.

"This lady stole from me, and I have every intention of taking her back to Missouri to pay."

"By marrying her?" Mr. Potter asked puzzled. Jubal clearly hadn't thought through his plan very well.

"You can't kidnap me," I said.

"But I can take what's mine."

"Nothing I have is yours," I said. With that, he lunged for our wagon as if to search it, but Edward grabbed him. Then our guide took him and tied his hands, "You're coming with me."

Our guide was able to find the sheriff and turned Jubal over to him.

Now we are free of Jubal! He won't bother us again if he's locked up in Salt Lake City for some time. I will sleep so well tonight knowing I'm freed of that burden. Edward was such a strong protector. He makes my heart leap with joy to know I'll be safe in his arms.

Tomorrow we're on our way again,

Love always,

Cora

November 3, 1856

Dear Lillian,

I'm sorry I haven't written since we stopped in Salt Lake City. It's so much easier to write sitting at a desk in a cabin than trying not to spill ink in a rocking wagon. I haven't known what to say, and have felt slightly embarrassed about what I am going to write. I preface by saying that if you were here, you would understand, but since you aren't you probably will think I'm a little crazy. Or impulsive. That's what you would say, but you always call me impulsive. You know I needed to escape Missouri. I am happy to say it's been a success. I'm thousands of miles away from you, my sister, in the most beautiful land you could ever imagine.

I'll begin with that. We've finally made it to California. It's like everything described to me, but not anything I could have ever imagined up in my own head. The trees here are enormous, larger than anything you've seen in your lifetime. Even the pine trees up in Maine can't compare. I haven't seen any gold yet, but Edward has. Some men still pan for gold in the river about ten miles south of our cabin.

Our cabin is small by eastern standards, but suites us fine. It's two rooms, made of logs, there's plenty of lumber out here. I have mama's cooking pots in the kitchen. I hang them over our hearth. We have piles of straw for the kids to sleep on in the loft. When I get some fabric I'll sew covers, make straw tick mattresses, but for now, we need the blankets as covers. So far, it's not as cold as Missouri, which suites me just fine. I've heard summers can be just as hot or hotter, but I've always loved summer sunshine, so I think I will handle it fine. Our cabin. You're probably teeming with curiosity now, so I'll go ahead and say it.

I've gone and done exactly what you told me not to do when I responded to his letter. I married him. But you have to admit it was inevitable. All the months on the trail, taking care of his children, it was bound to happen. Everyone knew it, and I think even you did as well. I'm sure you could even sense it. Couldn't you? I fell in love with the children first. After that, well, I started to notice Edward's heart for the children. No one else was going to love his children as much as me, and I think that softened him toward me. He is a tough man, there's no question about it, but he has a softer side too. It took a while, but I could see it more and more.

Don't hate me for not telling you sooner. I just couldn't bring myself to. Remember the celebration I mentioned on the shore of the Great Salt Lake? That was our wedding. So, when Edward told Jubal he was my husband, it was the truth.

I needed to know everything would work out. I don't regret any of my decisions, so I'm asking you to please forgive me for not telling you straight away. I also hope one day you'll be able to come visit us. Until then, please forgive me,

Always, your sister,

Cora

City of Angels

Ingrid Alice Lohr

Her lips parted, chapped, cracking and issued forth a single word, "No." She willed herself to take another step. The sun was just rising over the chalky cliffs that surrounded her.

She pressed the heels of her hands into the hallows of her eyes and screamed. Her knees gave out beneath her, weighed down by her failure and her foolish desires. Anton had been right all along. On hands and knees, she crawled forward to the edge of the cliff to gaze down into the empty, burned out valley below. The yellow heat rising in the distance promised another day of mind-numbing heat, beyond that, only the endless nothingness she had burned the souls of her feet on in the hopes of finding The Green Place, the City of Angels.

The wasteland, the gorge that lay before her where a great promised land should have been, was only an endless expanse of bleached out blue sky and grey, haunted desert.

No promised land.

No opportunity.

No new life.

No freedom.

Slowly, she laid her face in the dust and coughed, closed her eyes feeling the last cool shadows of the cliff, the desperate thirst in the earth waiting to drink her up when she passed.

In the silence of the desert, she heard it, the unmistakable sound, the 'Shhhcht, clink, shhhcht, clink' of the Wolf.

He had found her, even here.

A bolt of panic shot through her, hot and numbing, paralyzing her with fear.

"Johanna," the Wolf's voice was the same; gravel on the surface, rolling deep in black velvet. The very voice that followed her through every nightmare and spoke her darkest fears in her ear whenever she felt doubt creep in.

Johanna's eyes snapped open, turning her face to meet his figure—hulking and tall, left shoulder raised up higher than the right. The wide brim of his hat concealed the mess of his scared face, but no shadow could hide the piercing eyes beneath it. No dark or secret place existed that they could not penetrate within her. She could hide nothing from him.

She felt a tear slip from the corner of her upturned eye and dry before it reached her chin, "Please, no more, no more," her voice was strange to her, a rough whisper that tore at the parchment of her dry throat.

A gritty laugh issued from the Wolf's throat, filling up the valley, resonating off the cliffs.

He knelt beside her, giving her a full view of his mangled face, cleanly shaven now for the heat, "I told you, Johanna. I would find you. When you run from me, we play a game. My reward is your final breath," his lips pulled back to reveal his pointed teeth in a snarling grin.

Johanna struggled to push herself away from him, but his massive hands were on her in a flash, his face in hers, lips pressing over her scream, pulling it out, pulling out the air from her lungs. The raw taste of blood, salty and metallic filled her mouth, something else too filled it, tasting of tar. Her mind was thrown into bright popping flashes and dark reliefs, like the deep black spaces between the stars.

The stars.

The stars hung, always the same way, everywhere, even in her childhood. Bright and full of promise as she stood wrapped in her Papa's warm woolen jacket that smelt of wood smoke from the hearth, the thick animal smell of the barn and the wet cold of snow. She'd wanted to spend her last night at home, looking up at the stars. Her brothers had gone to the city already, her little sister growing thinner every day as her cough grew deeper and deeper, keeping everyone up at night.

The deep snow crumpled around her feet, soaking deep through her shoes into her stockings.

Her Papa's warm hand fell on her shoulder, he knelt beside her and pointed upward, "Do you see, my little doll, that brightest one in the sky?"

Johanna nodded.

"That star will always guide you. It will always take you home, no matter where you are," he told Johanna.

"Even in America, Papa?" Johanna asked.

Her Papa's face was worn thin now. Once, she could remember his round cheeks always ruddy from a days work in the fields, as he worked with the livestock. Now the pigs were all dead. Eaten away from the inside from worms, falling like skeletons in the snow and piled beside the barn until the thaw. The smile he gave his daughter was weak. He pulled his coat tighter around his daughter in the cold, "Yes, always. The stars are magic; they will always lead you on your path."

Johanna clung to the inside of the coat and looked back up at the stars. They seemed so small; even the brightest one seemed too small to be so magical. There was so much between them that held nothing.

"What are they?"

Tilting his head upward, Papa let out a musing sigh, "Wishes. Promises. Dreams. All the good things," he turned back to his daughter, transfixed on the specks of light in the night sky, "It's cold. You have a long journey ahead of you. It's time to go to sleep."

Her last night at home, Johanna hardly slept. Her mind raced with all the possibilities that awaited her. The small case she packed contained all her worldly possessions. Her nicest dress, the hand mirror and comb with inlaid mother of pearl, and a little yarn doll named Anna. They were the only things she had to take, the best things, the most precious things she owned. Johanna thought of how they would look next to all the new things her Aunt and Uncle would give to her once she arrived in the distant and mystical city of New York. She imagined all the wonderful things her Mutti and Papa told her of America, all the magnificent things the letter from her new benefactors contained. She would drink from real crystal glasses, eat off real china plates, with real silver forks and knives. Her room would be large, larger than the small cottage she shared with her family and filled with dresses, hats, scarves, mittens and fine kidskin gloves like nice girls wore.

She would be a princess in America.

When morning came, the snow came down wet and heavy. The approaching cart cut deep brown tracks into the road as it approached the cottage. In the doorway of the home, Johanna's Mutti wiped at her tears, holding her daughter tight, unwilling for the final goodbye. Stiffly, her Papa loosened his wife's grip on her, bringing her to the cart and lifting her in. His lips pressed together tightly.

"Papa?" Johanna searched his face for some sign of her fate as well as his.

"It is for the best," he said and kissed her, "Goodbye, my beautiful doll. We will always love you, never forget," he blinked hard once, and turned away from her. Her Papa slapped the side of the cart, signally the man to drive on.

"Papa!" Johanna cried out, throwing herself forward. At the same moment, the cart lurched forward and threw her back. She watched as her family and home became obscured by the falling snow. Johanna slid back, burying her face in her knees and cried, deep wails rang out from her until the man up front called back to her.

"Hey, hey, girl," he shouted from his perch.

Johanna let her crying die out, becoming a quiet mewling, but made no answer.

The cartman was quiet for a moment before he continued, "Where you are going, you will not be hungry or freeze. There are no beasts to snatch you from the forest at night and devour you. You can become a fine young woman," he spoke with a thick accent she could not identify and wondered, briefly, where he was from and how he knew these things about her.

She pretended not to hear him, and the man seemed not to care whether she spoke or didn't.

On their way to the port, the cart picked up two young men and a family with a young child. They were all headed to the same dream, yet they spoke little to each other on their way. At night Johanna poked her head out of the cart and looked for the bright star. It was easy to find, somehow, always above her. It made her smile.

"Let them be all right," she whispered to the star.

In Hamburg, the travelers climbed down off the cart, weary and sore. Chimneys belched black, acrid-smelling smoke. The streets were crowded with more people than Johanna had ever seen in her life. While the others busied themselves with their cases, the Cart Man pulled Johanna aside by her elbow.

"Your parents said you had a letter, let me see it," the Cart Man said.

Johanna blinked up at him, pulling the letter from her pocket.

The man nodded slowly as he read, "Do you know what this says?"

Johanna had tried to discern what it said but was unable to read the English words. Her parents had had to call the teacher from down the road to translate it to them when they'd received it. They had given it to her to carry with her as proof of who she was, but she did not know, precisely what it said.

She shook her head.

"Do you speak, girl, or just nod like a dumb animal?" the Cart Man snapped.

"I can speak just fine, I don't read any English," she shot back at him.

The man's face went tight, then broke into a smile, and he laughed, "Such a spirit. You are well suited for America, so let me help you. I know of your Uncle. He is the one who paid me to collect you. When you go to America, you must tell the man at the desk to send word for Theodor Brand. Tell the man 'My name is Mary Hill, I am from Hamburg, and I must have word sent to my Uncle Theodor Brand,' here now, let me hear you say that back, just like I did. English," he bobbed his finger at her and made her repeat the phrase back to him, twice. He handed her a small pack of papers and a necklace.

"What is all this?"

"The necklace is a gift from your Uncle, and the papers are for the man at the desk to see," he nodded to the necklace. It was gold with a small, single diamond. The sight of it catching in the dim light made Johanna's heart dance.

"It's so ... beautiful."

"A beautiful gift for a beautiful girl. Your Uncle trusted me to bring you here safely. Many times people do not make it. They get abandoned, or all their money is taken, and they have to stay here with no one and nothing. You're Uncle paid me well to make sure. Now put on the necklace, but hide it under your dress," he patted Johanna roughly on the head and pointed her to the docks and the queue forming without another word.

The ship towered over her, enormous and imposing, but below deck the room she shared with ten others was cramped. All her time was spent in her bunk, pouring over the mysterious papers and the letter. A woman in her room sat with her on some nights and let her look at the Bible she carried.

The woman told her it was the King James and written in English.

Johanna tried hard to listen to the woman speak the words and look at the writing at the tip of the woman's finger, desperate to learn what she could to impress her Uncle.

She dreamed of him, how impressed he would be when she got off the ship and could greet him in English. She also dreamed of the grand dinners they would all have together, the lovely walks under old trees in the parks and vases full of flowers she and her Aunt would pick from the garden.

While everyone slept, Johanna would pull the necklace out and hold it between her forefinger and thumb, whispering to it until she finally fell asleep.

On the ship, she lived in a near fog of other people. Low murmurs of conversations, people getting sick and fighting interrupted every moment. Shadows danced and drifted in the night taking on strange new shapes. Days passed into weeks until she thought she might have died, this was purgatory, and soon she would be called up for judgment or thrown into the pit.

Finally, a cry went out. America was in sight, and the news flitted through the cabins. Time passed no quicker. More hours and days she spent, shuffled from the boat to buildings and rooms and benches while she waited, drifting in and out of nightmarish sleep where all she could see were the monsters her mother warned her about in the faces of the other travelers. Lines stretched on forever. She never knew what or who she waited for until she stood before a little man with a shock of grey hair and black beetle eyes.

At his desk, he held a pen over a large ledger and spoke at her.

Groggy, Johanna could only stare at him. She'd forgotten what she was supposed to tell the desk man.

"Name!" the man drew out the word pointing at her.

Slowly her words began to take shape in her mind, "My name is Mary Hill, I am from Hamburg, My—"

The desk man held up his hand, stopping her, and jotted something into this book. He held out the same hand to her, "Papers, Miss Hill," he bit off the last word as if it was meant to insult her.

Johanna tried again, "I am from Hamburg, my Uncle is Theodor Brand."

He ignored her, scribbling in his book, muttering to himself. He sniffed loudly, put his pen down and thrust the papers back at Johanna.

"My Uncle," Johanna said to him.

He blinked at her and pointed toward the large doors opposite, "Welcome to America, Miss Mary Hill, may God Bless you," there was no trace of a smile on his face or in his words. Stunned, Johanna staggered toward the doors and out into the City of New York.

The chaos of the crowd outside overwhelmed Johanna with sound and the constant press of other bodies. Men approached her, asking her questions she did not understand, others stood before carts of apples or other wares tempting passers-by. Families lugged their boxes and cases through the crowd, searching out transport or relatives.

All around her there were only strangers.

How was she supposed to find her Uncle? Had she missed him? Was she forgotten?

Desperate and frantic she spotted a group of boys close to her age. Wiping away her welling tears she approached them, repeating her lines. When they said nothing and merely turned away from her, her tears finally broke loose.

"Stupid girl," she heard an old woman's voice behind her and turned. Dressed in black with a shawl to protect her from the drizzle the wizened faced woman glared at Johanna with the eyes of the hawk.

"I need to find my Uncle," Johanna told the woman. She was relieved to finally be speaking to someone who understood her, no matter how frightful the woman's appearance was.

The old woman threw her hands up at the girl, "Silly, foolish girl! Where are your parents, why do they send you all alone?"

"To meet my Uncle," Johanna repeated, "His name is Theodore Brand, he's very wealthy and sent for me."

"No one's Uncle just meets them here. It's a long voyage, here, I'll take you back in to speak to the men inside, they'll find a place for you," the old woman's bony hand snapped out and gripped Johanna's wrist, digging in. The girl pulled back, frightened of the cold, sharp press of the woman's fingers.

Johanna shook her head. She didn't want to go back in and speak with the little man or anyone like him. She feared where they might put her.

"Young lady!" From the crowd another voice, a familiar dialect issued. Johanna turned and spotted the young man who was calling, "Young lady, please, wait," he was a few years older than she, with dark blond hair and deep, kind brown eyes. He fixed her with a smile. He looked like a prince from one of the fairytales her Mutti would read to her before bed.

"Yes, sir?" Johanna asked.

"Shoo, go away," the old woman snarled at the young man.

He paid no attention, stepping in front of the hunched woman, offering his hand to Johanna, "Did you say you were looking for your Uncle? Mister Theodore Brand?"

"Yes," Johanna cried.

"You must be the niece he sent for?"

"Yes, I'm Johanna."

"My name is Tomas. I'd be pleased to take you to your Uncle; he'll be glad to know you have arrived safely."

The old woman scoffed, "Why doesn't he meet his niece himself," she muttered. Johanna felt, again, the old woman's claw on her wrist, "Don't go with this little rat."

Tomas cast a sharp stare on the woman. He reached out and removed the old woman's hand, putting a protective arm around Johanna, and turning her away from the woman, "Don't listen to her, young Johanna. She'd rob you blind if turned your back on her."

The old woman made a sound of irritation, throwing her hands up, "Foolish girl," she snapped and spat on the ground at the pair as they escaped from her into the crowd. Johanna's heart swelled. It was a miracle, in her darkest hour to be discovered by this kind and handsome young man. Her Papa had been right, America was the land of luck and hope.

Johanna found herself staring at the towering buildings, the people buying and selling all manner of foods and wares on the streets and in the shop windows.

"Tomas, what does my Uncle do?"

Tom let his face fall into a wide smile, "A little of everything."

"What do you do for him?"

"Mind his affairs and investments. See to his property. I'm meant to teach you English too, do you know any?"

Johanna shook her head, "Oh, only a little from a woman on the ship. She told me the Lord's Prayer."

"Your Uncle speaks English, he knows French and also some Russian. It helps him in his business."

"Does he run a shop?"

Tomas shrugged, "He is a very smart man. Don't be scared of how he looks. Do as he says and he'll take care of you. He took care of me when I was just little and now, well, you see?"

"Yes, Tomas," Johanna said admiring the way he carried himself. The people seemed to part for him without effort.

"Good," Tomas said and smiled again, leading her further into the city until they came to a tall stone building. They went down a set of steep, narrow steps to a large wooden door where Tomas knocked.

A barked word was uttered from inside, and the door opened a crack. Dark eyes looked them up and down before it was thrown open to reveal another boy who allowed them to enter.

The room was large, packed from floor to ceiling with furniture. Little tables crowded around chairs and sofas with piles of soft cushions. Paintings and drapes in deep reds with gold filigree hung on the windowless walls. Across from the door a fireplace crackled against the cold, a pot of something filling the air with a delicious aroma of stewing meat, onion, and root vegetables caused Johanna a pang of hunger so great that her stomach rumbled loudly in the quiet of the room.

So enthralled was she by the room she hadn't noticed the man by the fire until he gave out a gruff bark of a laugh as he turned toward her and from the light.

His eyes were the clearest, palest blue Johanna had ever seen, set in a face that was crisscrossed with scars where it wasn't hidden by a thick black beard and head of long curly hair.

The man smiled at her, without showing his teeth.

"Your niece, Johanna, sir," Tomas said in a formal tone as he pressed the small of the girls' back to push her forward into the light of the many candles and fireplace.

"My dear Johanna," her Uncle said rising out of his chair, stretching out his arms, "Come, give your Uncle a big hug and kiss."

Slowly Johanna crossed the room and fell forward into the man's arms.

"No kiss?" he asked, pointing to his scarred cheek. His eyes were sharp on her, dancing light from the fire turned their paleness yellow.

Johanna stood on tiptoe and laid a quick kiss on his rough cheek.

Her Uncle collapsed back into his chair and pulled the girl into his lap, "You are how old now, my niece?"

"I will be fourteen soon."

"Do you speak any English?"

"She doesn't know much, sir," Tomas said, "I can teach her."

Her Uncle tilted his head at the boy, "Oh yes?"

Tomas nodded.

"Tom will teach you then, my Johanna. He will teach you all you need to know."

Johanna knit her brows together, "Where is my Aunt?"

Across the room, Tom cleared his throat. Her uncle held the boys gaze in silence for a long, tense moment Johanna could not understand.

"Oh my sweet girl, she passed away from this world a few weeks ago."

Johanna thought she should cry, but having never known the woman, she could not summon the emotion. Instead, she nodded solemnly and leaned in to give the man another hug. He patted the girl affectionately on the back and took her hands in his admiringly, "Such fine little hands. The hands of a real lady," he smiled at her, the tips of his teeth poking out, looking very sharp to her eye, "Now, Tom will show you to bed. In the morning, there is much to learn if this city is to provide your future."

Her Uncle tipped her from his lap and patted her on the head. Tomas came forward and took her hand in his, warm and soft. He lead her to a small door hidden behind a curtain and up a set of rickety stairs.

Johanna, after hearing all of her parents dreams of what her life would be like in America was expecting a grand room, large bed and changing table laid out with all manner of brushes and perfumes. At the top of the stairs, Tomas threw open a door on a dull, grey room. A broken down sofa stood against one wall and a chair with a basin, a little table with a candle, nothing more. The wind from outside made the single window rattle in its frame.

"I thought," Johanna began.

Tomas narrowed his eyes at her, "Your Uncle is an excellent businessman. In the morning I will teach you," he walked across the room and patted the sofa, "Now sit down. I'll bring you up something to eat."

Tomas was true to his word, bringing her a bowl of stew and slice of dry bread and a glass of something dark colored and sharp smelling, telling her it would help her sleep. She ate the stew, using the bread to sop up the liquid and drank down the glass in a single swallow. Soon she was feeling sleepy and was curling beneath the itchy pile of blankets, drifting far down into a dreamless sleep.

The first morning came in dim and gray, filtered through the filthy piece of cloth tacked to the small window. Johanna's head felt swollen and heavy.

There was a pounding at the door, Tomas' faint voice came through the thick wood, "It's time to get up, Johanna. Time to learn."

Johanna fumbled around on the floor, pulled her discarded dress on and crossed the room to open the door. Tomas stood leaning against the door frame. Behind him the dark-eyed boy stood with his arms folded across his chest, a sullen look on his face, his cheek swelling yellow and purple beneath his left eye.

Tomas looked her up and down and nodded toward the stairs, "The Wolf taught me everything I know. We will play a game today, but first, we must teach you the rules."

Puzzled, Johanna frowned, "Who is the Wolf?"

"Ah," Tomas snorted a laugh and turned his gaze to her, "I mean, your Uncle. He's my Uncle and Anton's as well," he gestured toward the boy behind her on the stairs.

"We are cousins? I don't understand," Johanna put her hand to her head, pressing her fingers to her eyes.

Tomas sneered, "The Wolf is Uncle to us all. We are his children. If we want a happy home, we earn our keep. We are a family, a pack."

"I ... I don't understand," Johanna repeated.

"No need to understand. Just learn."

Tomas's game was simple to learn.

Johanna would stand on the corner, holding a box of flowers to sell, waiting for a well-dressed man to pass by. When he did, she tipped the box over and started crying, pointing helplessly to the strewn flowers around his feet. Most times a crying girl was enough but when it wasn't Anton or Tomas emerged from a doorway and started shouting, boxing Johanna around the ears until the mark paid up.

There were other games, too. The boys taught her how to be invisible, able to brush against people and pull a purse out of a pocket. Anton showed her how to distract the fruit sellers long enough so he could lift two apples off the cart for a special treat they could eat in the park. With his pocket knife, he cut the apples in half and showed her the star made by the seeds inside.

The boys pointed out everything in the markets, showed her all the buildings and taught her all the English words for the things they showed her. She loved to look at the good-looking young men and woman, the shops of lacy dresses and delicate pastries in the windows.

Tomas would take Johanna to help him collect on the debts owed to the Wolf whenever she was being too troublesome and fussy or asked too many questions. The neighborhoods where debts were owed were always cramped, pigs in the street among the drunks and whores, the stink of garbage thrown out of hovel windows caused Johanna to feel sick. He liked to show her just what could befall her.

"See how well he takes care of you, of us?" Tomas asked her stepping over a drunk laying prone in a stairwell.

A year passed.

Johanna came to understand the first game she ever played, though she hadn't known her part in it at the time. Tomas called it hunting. He taught her how to look for the right kind of child, the kind who was too wide-eyed, lost, asking questions to the wrong sorts of people. Once they'd said it, that they were looking for their Uncle, to approach them, to miraculously find their little cousin, their employer's new ward or older brother's long lost child.

"It doesn't always work," Tomas said as they sat on the wall, eating a lunch of bread and cold sausages he'd brought for them.

"Only fools fall for it?" Johanna asked.

Anton was out in the crowd, waiting, listening, hunting. Tomas shrugged his shoulders watching the other boy, "Innocents," he corrected then raised his chin, "Look."

Johanna followed the direction Tomas indicated. It was the old, hunched woman again, her hand held out to beg, "She tried to warn me," Johanna said gritting her teeth.

Tom shook his head, "She's one of the Wolf's. She owes him her life, same as us. Poor old thing drinks every penny she earns. He'll have to collect from her soon."

Johanna watched as Anton approached the woman. Without looking at her, he dropped a few coins into her outstretched hand. The old woman slipped them into her pocket. Johanna's lips tightened into a grimace. A few coins here and there would never be enough for the Wolf, but there was always a way to make payment to him. She swallowed hard thinking about the nights she'd slipped down into the Wolf's room, snooping around and finding odd pieces of meat wrapped in cloth and glass bottles filled with viscus dark liquid that glowed red against the glass in the firelight.

Johanna shook her head and returned to looking at Tomas.

This America, this city was not the paradise she had dreamed of all the long hours and days and weeks she'd spent in travel. It was no beautiful dream, but there *were* opportunities, Papa had been right about that.

Johanna tried not to think of her family. It was easier. She knew there were places in this land that were what her parents dreamed, but it was not this city. Somewhere beyond, there were wide open places with clear blue skies and emerald pastures.

Anton told her about those places. He kept pamphlets and posters hidden in his room and let Johanna look at them whenever she cried over the grey room, the trash-filled streets and dead-eyed women sporting bruised eyes and split lips.

He told her someday he'd save enough money and go West, raise horses, sleep in a big house and breath clean air.

"I'll get away from him, someday," Anton told her, blotting his bleeding nose. He could have been the Wolf's son. The same dark, curling hair, angular cheeks set high on his face, and broad shoulders that were scared and misshapen in the Wolf were innocent and soft in Anton. He received no special treatment for it. Johanna was the Wolf's jewel, always under his and Tomas's watchful eye.

Tomas searched her room often, dragging her down to the basement for the Wolf to instruct her.

Rising stiffly from his chair the Wolf would cross the room, his foot dragging a little, hissing over the floorboards, his other step heavy, thumping out an irregular beat before his thick hands would come down on her shoulders. He would smile at her, careful about his teeth.

"Let me show you something," he told her pointing to a scar on his face, "I got this for a lie."

He pointed out all the scars. The ones for keeping money from his father, spending too much time daydreaming, forgetting to close the gate to the pigs' pen. The last thing he would point to was his leg, "I told my father I wanted to go to school like the rich boys and tried to run from home," one eyebrow lifted on his scared face.

From the corner of her eye, Johanna would watch Tomas rolling up his sleeve to reveal three broad brands, each one made by the poker from the fire. After the third time, Tom never tried to run again.

"You understand," the Wolf smiled, knowing what she saw, knowing she could still feel the sear of the iron on her skin from the first time she tried to run.

"Not too many options for a young woman like yourself in this world," he moved around back to his desk with the hiss, thump, hiss thump of his steps back to this desk, "Better to stay with your family and not have silly dreams."

Still, Johanna could not stop herself from dreaming. She hated the games she had to play to earn a living and found herself wandering more frequently away from her corners, Anton, trailing behind her, his hands finding their way into other people's pockets to fill their quota.

More often than not they came up short, unable to account for both their dues, Anton pressed all the money into Johanna's palms and went down into the basement to face the Wolf alone.

When he discovered how Johanna spent her afternoons, Tomas told the Wolf, and he sent for her. In his chamber, Anton stood in the middle of the room as the Wolf circled the boy. He kept his eyes trained on the girl's face, "How can you do this to your family?" he asked Anton, "Do you want us all to starve while you laze around town doing nothing but dreaming of your horses and railroads? You disappoint me, Anton," his voice came up like a rumble from his chest. He pulled up his sleeves, drawing back and striking the boy, over and over until he fell to the floor.

Anton made no sound. He did not cry out and when it was over the Wolf patted him on the shoulder, "Good boy. You pay your debt like a man."

Johanna's hatred deepened. She snuck up to the roof with Anton to look up at the night sky.

She pointed up at the stars, "Each one is a dream, a promise," she told him.

"Which one is yours?" Anton asked.

"They all are," Johanna told him.

Anton stretched out a hand, touching Johanna's wrist with a single finger. She turned her hand, palm up and laced her fingers through his hand.

They decided to leave on a Sunday.

Tickets purchased, they packed two ruck-sacks and slipped away from the Wolf's den in the middle of the night.

On the train, Anton and Johanna were just another young couple searching out a better life in the West. Together they watched as the landscape changed, flattened out to meet the horizon.

Johanna let herself dream again.

She cared for Anton, but was not in love with him, though he certainly was with her. She watched young mothers in the car, caring for their children and felt no pang of desire for motherhood. Even if that was the hand she was inevitably delt when they came to Courtland.

They should have pressed on, gone with the teams of wagons to brave the desert and native raiders who would just as soon scalp you as look at you, if the other travelers were to be believed. They decided to stay the night in a little room above the tavern.

In the night, the men came. Johanna heard them downstairs at the bar, shouting, then heard the noisy footfalls on the stairs. Anton sprang from the bed and ran to meet the commotion. A shot rang out, when he came back he locked the door. Blood stained his shirt, "We should not have stayed here," he said pulling off his soiled clothes. He set a pistol down on the bed. Johanna's eyes fixed on it. She picked it up.

It might be easier to move on alone she thought, "He found us?"

"Maybe men he hired, I saw them on the train, but I thought," Anton stopped, his dark eyes settling on the pistol in Johanna's hand.

"Why would he do this? Go through all the trouble?"

She knew the answer.

Anton crossed the room, picking up her bag he threw it onto the floor unopened before her feet. He ran a hand through his dark hair and smirked. He picked up his bag and set it down next to hers, pulling it open to show her what was inside, "I didn't think you would have it in you."

"We stole a lot from him," Johanna mused. She let out a laugh.

"We've got to run. He'll want to collect," Anton answered.

"He'll want to kill us."

"If he can catch us."

"Some women on the train were talking about this big city through the desert. If you go far enough, there is green, and no one cares where you come from," Johanna held her arms up, "You find the two big pillars and there it is."

Anton shook his head, "They're talking about a fairy tale, it's not a real place. There's no place we can hide for long; there never will be. We have to try," Anton pulled a clean shirt on, "Quick, get dressed."

The commotion from down the stairs offered them just enough cover to slip out of the tavern, untether a pair of horses and ride out along the road.

The sky was so dark, as dark as the skies from when she was a girl. Johanna tipped her head back and gazed up at the canopy of stars. They went on forever, stretching out and out into the desert, drawing her forever on. They rode on for two days before they saw an abandoned homestead and knew another town was close.

By nightfall, they arrived at the town of Pearce. The Inn at the end of the Main Street lent them a room and asked no questions of the young couple. A piano played in the tavern, just audible above the roar of conversation, laughter, and shouting. The patrons were crowded in, clustered in little groups around tables, playing cards and drinking beer at the bar. No one looked in their direction, they were invisible, and for a moment Johanna felt safe among the strangers.

In the morning Anton got a job in a hardware store and left Johanna to pass the days in the strange new land by herself. She walked up and down the street, looking in on the shops. The women who worked at the brothel were friendly to her. They asked her where she'd come from and how long she had been married.

"Any little ones?" Bernadette asked pushing her mess of bright red hair up off her face.

The heat was something Johanna could never get used to. It seemed the other ladies coped with it by drinking glass after glass of beer in their afternoons before work.

"No," Johanna told them, "Have you ever heard of the city past the White Pillars?"

Bernadette cocked a half smile, "You should talk to Anna about that city. She calls it the City of Angels. She and some of the other girls like to talk about getting there someday when they're older."

Johanna's face lit up, "So it's real? Anton said it was just a story."

Bernadette laughed and took another swig of her beer, "Oh, it's real alright, more real than anything else around."

"How do we get there?"

The woman shrugged, "There are lots of ways, some easier than others. Anna always says she'll find it once this town has worn her out, she'll just walk out into the desert and follow the sky until she finds it."

Whether it was her drinking that made it hard for Johanna to completely understand her or not, she endeavored to keep asking. At night Johanna would watch the men go in and out of the brothel and the saloons, stumbling out drunk into the streets, brawling openly. It was the only time she ever saw a man shot, though he didn't die. Both were drunk and fought over a woman outside the general store when one pulled a gun, aimed it with shaky hands and pulled the trigger, striking the man in the shoulder. Three other men rushed him before he was able to get another shot off and he spent the night in jail, raving and shouting out his love's name until the sun came up.

Johanna began to have dreams of the Wolf. They were always the same.

He followed her into every landscape, beneath a sky empty of stars. In a forest she would hear quick footsteps behind her, turn and see nothing. In the empty desert, she could hear the wind whistling faster and faster, kicking up clouds of dust to obscure her vision.

Then from nowhere, his hands were on her, his face in her's, demanding and shouting out, "You owe me, girl, you owe me your very life. You stole it from me, and I will get it back."

His mouth would open, unhinging like the snakes in the shadows of the sand worn buildings revealing only darkness that swallowed up her screams.

It started to happen, the eyes were on her again in the general store, or in the back of the church, but when she turned around, nothing.

"I want to try and find the Valley," she told Anton again, "I'm afraid here."

Anton paused from shaving in the small mirror above the chair where he set the wash basin, "Johanna," he sighed, "There's no such place. We're safe here, we've been safe here for months. Don't you like it here?"

"No," Johanna said. She hadn't the heart to tell him about the letter that had come for her. The Innkeeper handed it to her across the bar. She could not read what the words said on the card, but she could guess who it was from. In their room, she slipped it beneath the mattress and only took it out when Anton was not around, to try and figure out the two words written there.

After the church service, a blonde woman stood in the shadow of the church looking at Johanna. Her face was set hard, rough from the endless sun. She walked with a strangely wide gate when she approached the girl.

"You Johanna?" The woman asked.

She nodded, stepping back.

"Anna," the woman said pointing to herself, "You come here to work or disappear?"

"Neither," Johanna answered.

Anna snorted out a weak laugh, then coughed, "That's not true. No one comes here, just to come here. Bernie said you've been asking a lot of questions about the City, that true?"

"It is."

Anna shook her head, "I was born on a farm. My daddy beat me every day of my life, so I came here. Here is where I first heard of it, but it's not a place for you. Don't bother asking anyone else about it."

Johanna licked her dry lips and shaded her eyes from the early afternoon sun, "I heard people talk about it in Courtland when we first came west."

Anna nodded, "Some women know where it is, but trust me, it's no place for you to go."

Johanna blinked, "Why not?"

"You ask too many questions. That isn't good out here. You stand out if you do that and something tells me, you'd rather hide."

"What about the Pillars? My Papa told me once you could follow a star—"

"Just stop asking," Anna cut her off sharply, "Have a good day, Johanna."

She walked slowly away from her down the street and into the brothel. Johanna stopped herself from following.

A second envelope came three days after she encountered Anna. Instead of opening it downstairs in front of the innkeeper she went up to their room. Tucked inside with the card with more writing a tuft of musty hair fell out onto the floor. She bent down and picked it up between her forefinger and thumb. It felt gritting and oily. Two more words were on the card. Johanna placed the card and hair with the other and decided to go to the Imperial Saloon by herself.

Johanna entered the saloon feeling the usual pause in conversation as the patrons took notice of her. She took a seat facing the door, near the corner of the Saloon and watched the crowd. All the faces, all the different faces from all the ends of the earth, talking together, weaving a tapestry of meaningless sound. She waited to feel the eyes on her, waited to see a familiar face peering at her. There was a stillness in the crowd that let her think more clearly.

From the other side of the Saloon, a bottle smashed. She jumped, her eyes going to the source of the disturbance. Two men stood chest to chest over a game of cards, they grabbed each other and began tumbling around on the floor knocking over chairs as they did.

Johanna slipped out and walked down to the end of the street and stood at the edge of the desert. For a long time she felt alone, then she heard the approach of footsteps and felt Anton place a hand on her shoulder.

"It's late," he told her, "Did you get to eat any dinner?"

Johanna shook her head.

"You should eat. I feel like you are getting thin."

She nodded and turned away from him to look back into the flat expanse beyond the town.

In the morning, Johanna decided she would ask someone to read the notes. She concluded if Anton would not leave and trust that she did not feel safe, she would leave on her own. She tucked the cards into her waistband and went down to the General Store.

She paced in the aisles, holding her hand to the place where she kept the cards. She was unable to bring herself to let another see them. By the evening she had gone into every shop and still the cards remained hidden, and a mystery. Johanna returned to the Inn to find a third envelope waiting for her. She stared at it, unopened on the polished bar. Slowly, hand trembling she reached out and opened the letter. Inside another card, with a single word on one side. When she turned it over, there was a single spot of blood.

"Who sent this?" Johanna croaked out.

The innkeeper shrugged, "Blond man brought it over."

Johanna reached for the other cards and laid them out on the bar, "Sir, what do these say?"

The man leaned over and looked at the two cards, "They say, 'Your Dreams Come True."

Johanna nodded slowly, "And this one?" she placed the last card down on the bar, blood stain down.

"Tonight," he smiled at her, "An admirer of yours?"

"Do you know the man who brought these?" Johanna asked.

He stopped polishing the glass in his hand and set it with the others, "Never seen him before. Nice looking young fellow, very polite."

Johanna's breath caught in her throat; her blood turned to fire in her veins.

"Miss? Miss, you don't look so well, are you all right?" the innkeeper asked.

She tried to nod. Her ears felt like they were stuffed with cotton. She turned away from the bar and ran to the stairs climbing them as fast as she could. She stood outside the room for a long moment before turning the knob, letting the door fall open into the room.

Anton sat with his back to her, across from him Tomas slouched in the other chair, smirking.

"Hello, Johanna. Anton and I were just having a little talk," Tomas lifted his foot and shoved it hard against Anton's chair. He slumped forward, dropping face first to the floor. Johanna let out a gasp as he lay there, unsure if he was unconscious or dead.

"You have something that does not belong to you," Tomas said.

Johanna's heart thundered in her ears, she sidestepped toward the chest of drawers and heard the click of a pistol's hammer.

"Careful, Johanna," Tomas warned.

She froze. If he were going to shoot her, he would have. When he did not, she squared her shoulders and moved decisively for the bag shoved behind the chest of drawers. She threw it at him, "Here, just take it."

Tomas cocked his head to the side, not taking his eyes off the girl. He rose from his seat and stepped toward the bag, pistol still pointed at her and kicked the bag. His laugh was biting, "This is not what we came for."

He stepped over the bag coming to face her, "It's time to play the last game," he told her resting his free hand on her shoulder. He bent to whisper in her ear, "The Wolf is coming, time to run."

He laughed again, backing away from her. He picked up the bag and slung it over his shoulder. Johanna blinked, feeling sweat breakout all over. Tomas turned from her, shutting the door as he left.

Johanna's breath came rushing in all at once, in ragged crazed breaths. She ran to Anton. He was still breathing, though it was shallow. She had no time to wait. She had to leave. Quickly, she pushed back the bedframe and grabbed the remaining bag. She threw what little she had in with the remaining loot.

She could go farther; she could follow the desert until she found the white pillars and the emerald valley beyond it, the City of Angels.

Johanna wiped at her eyes, taking one last look around the room. She shoved the pistol from under the pillows down her dress and slipped from the room, down the stairs and out of town, out into the desert.

In the desert, there was no road to follow, and no one to meet. At night she listened to the howling of coyotes and traced the lines the stars made as though they were the map to the city. She felt thirst and hunger, exhaustion until the desert seemed to swallow those things from her and she no longer felt a need for them. As she walked she unburdened herself, leaving behind a trail of clothes, jewelry, and coins she'd taken from the Wolf until she carried only the things she needed. A set of matches to start her fire, the pistol and the clothes on her back. In the city, she would be able to have everything she had lost and more.

She finally laid down the pistol and took off her shoes and set them pointing back the way she'd come. Johanna stepped back and looked at them, dust-covered and worn thin.

She continued to walk into the setting sun.

In the night, Johanna stretched out and looked up into the sky and wondered how many days and nights she'd walked, how many more she would have to walk through the white coves she had discovered out here. If she squinted in the mornings, she could still make out the dark smudges left by the fires she'd built from the previous nights. It seemed she could walk all day and never get far enough, the sun managed to play tricks on her.

By the fire she could look out and see the cliffs opening up, creating a dark arrow with a single bright star hanging in the center of the gap. She would let that star bring her to her destination. She could outrun the Wolf if only she could make it to that star. It winked at her and whispered her to sleep with the list of her dreams and longings.

By morning, she knew, that star would lead her into the City. She could get to the gorge and find the green valley, the new city, and the life she craved.

The star was her protector, her silent warrior, it would lead her home.

Her eyes closed on the star, and when she re-opened them, she lay in the dust, the sand whipping at her, scratching her skin in the gray light. Johanna felt only the continual, dull ache she had for days as she stood and moved toward the parting in the white cliffs, patient to see what lay on the other side.

Dead Man Breathing

Jerome W. McFadden

I sat on the ridge waiting for the sun to come up. Old Henry nuzzled me on the shoulder as if anxious to get moving. The old pack mule was probably tired of being hobbled up and just wanted to move his legs and wander off to somewhere to scrounge for food. On the other hand, even a dumb animal could sense there was too much death in the camp behind us, and it was time to get the hell out of here.

Going or staying didn't matter. I was a dead man breathing. The waterhole smelled putrid. The standing water was opaque and white and brackish and tasted sour. It made me vomit if I drank too much. Even scrawny old Henry refused to drink out of it.

Great choice. Stay here and poison myself or pack up the stupid mule and move out—into an endless desert that had no water. Only burned out cactus and rock. Red rocks, brown rocks, and occasional black rocks, all scorched by the searing sun. It didn't matter in which direction I went. Just more of the same.

And that damn bunch of raggedy-ass Indians were still out there. *Probably watching me right now. Waiting to surprise me.* I had more guns than one man could use, three pistols and three rifles, but could only shoot one at a time. Maybe two pistols at a time, but how do you aim when you're shooting two pistols, and a bunch of damn Indians are swarming around you in front, back, and both sides? I ain't ever tried and don't want to find out.

How'd I get here?

It didn't start out bad.

John Rogers had a contract to move a hundred head of cattle out of El Paso to Fort Washington, north of Del Rio. Said he needed another hand. He had a good rider named Jameson and a half breed Indian who claimed to know the territory like the back of his hand. He even had a Chines cook called Chan who was gonna drive the chuck wagon, then move on to San Antonio to find a job.

Four riders with a well-supplied chuck wagon with a good cook oughta be able to handle a hundred head of cattle. But getting them from El Paso to Fort Washington might be a hard effort. "There ain't hardly enough grass out there to keep 'em fed," I said.

Rogers took off his hat to wipe his brow. The top half of his forehead was white from where the hat protected him from the sun, "We don't need to get them there fat," he said. "We just need to get them there. They're the army's problem after that."

So, I signed on. I was sick of El Paso. Been there a month. Too many cheats at the gambling tables and not enough new whores in the sporting houses. I was never cut out for working in a city. Too many people. Too many rules.

The only hesitation I had was when Rogers said we were going to cross the Apache Mountains.

"It's pretty well quieted down out there now," Rogers said. "A few roving bands here and there but they're getting them rounded up."

"Who says?"

Montés, the half breed, was standing beside Rogers. He spat on the ground and smiled at me like the smile hurt his face. "You 'fraid of a couple old 'pachés that don' know when to quit?"

He was short and stocky with skin the color of dark wood, with a nice scar running from the corner of his left eyebrow to his upper lip as if somebody tried to cut half his head off. He had a soiled bandanna wrapped around his forehead that looked like it hadn't been washed in the past two years.

"Four men and a cook riding a hundred cows into Apache country might make a tempting target to a couple of old Apaches that don't know when to quit."

Montés spat on the ground again and turned away from me. "We don' need you. Three of us can handle it."

I looked over at Rogers. "Who's running the show? You or him?"

"We need you, Marcus. You're a good cowhand, and you can shoot. I've seen you do it."

"Do you really need to go through those mountains?"

Rogers shrugged and stared out at the countryside at the edge of town. "It cuts off fifty miles, and the valleys are flat with a few watering holes. With a little luck, we can make it to Fort Washington with all one-hundred head."

"And all four of ours, too?"

"That's the plan."

So off we went. At the break of dawn. Out of the cattle yards north of El Paso. Rogers, Jameson, and I counted the cows, crowding them into a herd. They bawled and bellowed and acted frisky and ornery, still fresh with energy, but finally settled into a loose, bulky file. Montés rode far in front of us as if he had nothing to do with getting this operation started.

Chan came rolling out of town in the chuck wagon, lashing the two mules with his whip, waving and yelling at us as he hurried to catch up, the pots and pans clanging against the side boards.

The cows were plodding along straight and placid, so I dropped back to ride beside him. He was chubby and cheerful and looked to be the talkative type, which might be a nice change from the usual taciturn cowpokes that I rode with. Within two days of any ride, ten words around a campfire in the evening marked you as a social animal. "You sure you're riding with the right crowd?" I asked with a smile.

"You Malcus?"

"I'm Marcus," I replied, correcting him.

"Tha's wha' I say. Malcus."

He was dressed funny. A white cotton jacket with buttons and high collar, floppy pants, and a round hat that looked like the ones the cooks in some fancy restaurant might wear. His rickety old wagon sure as hell was not a fancy restaurant, and we didn't know yet how well he could cook.

"You know you're going to San Antonio the long way," I kidded.

"Need to work. Nothin' flee in this country."

Flee or flea? Big difference. I went with free, which made me laugh. "Tell me about it," I said. "Where you from?"

"China. I Chinaman."

"I can see that. From where in—"

Roger yelled at me, pointing at a heifer and her calf wandering off by themselves into a small arroyo. *Already? This might turn out to be a long trip.*

Damned if Chan couldn't cook. He was good. Real good. He made bacon and beans worth farting about. And spaghetti. I ain't never had spaghetti on a ride before. With meat sauce. He called them noodles. But we knew they were spaghetti. Jameson had never heard the word noodles before.

He even found the way into Montés' heart. The two of them would ride out in front of the herd all day scouting the route and looking for a campsite for the evening. Then while they were waiting for us, Chan would go out searching for snakes and lizards and finding wild onions and grasshoppers, and cactus pears.

But he was smart enough, in the beginning, not to tell us what we were eating. He'd have those snakes and lizards stripped and cut up and boiled or grilled by the time we arrived and mix all of it in with beans and toasted biscuits. Montés would eat his without the beans. Just the onions and cactus pears.

Then about the fourth night, Jameson asked, "What is this white stuff? It's damned good."

"Lattle snake," Chan said.

"What the hell is lattle snake?"

Montés grinned at him and answered for Chan, "Rattlesnake. He means rattlesnake."

Jameson went as white as the pallid strips of snake on his plate, then rose to his feet to walk outside of the firelight to vomit in the bushes.

Chan had a horrified look on his face. "You no want me to cook lattlesnake, no more?"

Rogers and I exchanged looks. We knew it wasn't bothering Montés any, and it as hell won't bother either one of us, so Rogers shook his head and spat on the ground and said, "Man's gotta eat."

The trouble started at the end of the first week. Something, or someone, spooked the herd. Rogers was riding the late-night watch and said he heard nothing, absolutely nothing, but all of a sudden, the herd took off like someone stuck a hot branding iron straight up their collective asses.

It took us at least two miles for the four of us to get them rounded up and settled back in, and we didn't have a clue where we were. Chan and his wagon caught up to us at dawn and made us a well-deserved breakfast.

The morning count said we lost ten cows.

We spent the morning looking for them but not a trace. Just another day wasted.

One of the mules disappeared the next night. "I had them hobbled," Chan protested. "Hobbled good. Andrew really tight. 'Cause he like to wander off. Old Henry not so much. He too old and want to rest at night."

"You named your mules?" Jameson asked in surprise.

"Sure, I name my mules. How I talk to them if I don't know their names."

"They're just ... mules."

"They work belly hard. They should have names."

Jameson walked off muttering to himself. But Rogers, I, and Montés looked at one another. We knew something was going on out there at night.

"Can you pull the wagon with only one mule?" Rogers asked Chan.

"Belly hard. Belly, belly hard. Old Henry belly old. Maybe you give me a cow to pull, too."

"You're gonna hitch a cow and mule to pull the wagon?"

"You got better idea?"

Which slowed us down further. The cow and mule were not a great team. And the country was getting harder. We had to cut back our distance per day to let Chan and his badly matched eight-legged crew catch up.

Montés disappeared the third night. Jameson was out riding watch. The half breed volunteered to stand watch around the camp while Rogers and I settled into our blankets. Chan was cleaning his pots and pans before climbing into his wagon to sleep.

In the morning, everything about him was gone. His blankets, his saddlebags, his horse, and his guns.

"This ain't right," Jameson said, visibly upset.

"But where he go?" Chan asked, bewildered.

I was the one who said it, "I think he just changed sides."

Rogers nodded, not speaking.

"D-Do we know how to get there from here? To Fort Washington, I mean?" Jameson asked.

"More or less," Rogers replied.

"Less than more," I added.

"Just as bad going back."

I shrugged. "They're waiting out there for us, either way we go."

Jameson did not like that comment. He apparently hadn't figured it out yet. "They? Waiting out there for us? Who the hell is out there waiting for us?"

"One of them roving bands the army hasn't brought in yet," I said.

"Probably," Rogers confirmed.

"And Montés just joined them?" Jameson said, red in the face.

"Probably," Rogers repeated.

"Or he cut bait and went home. Did the count and decided we were on the losing side," I added.

"So what are we gonna do?"

Rogers walked over to his horse to start saddling up but looked back at Jameson, "Keep on keeping on. Only thing we can do."

But we had to abandon the chuck wagon. It was too risky to have Chan trundling along way behind both the heard and us. Too exposed all by himself. So, we unloaded the wagon as best we could and packed it on old Henry and formed a bare spot between the bundles for Chan to ride on. Neither old Henry or Chan was happy about it, but at least Chan understood the situation.

The pattern began to change. A handful of cows would now disappear every other night. Rogers and I decided that the Apaches were herding them off bit by bit to a main camp not far away. No point in fighting us when they could whittle us to death.

The question then became if it was too dangerous for us to ride watch at night. An easy way to get picked off, one by one. And our patrolling around the herd was not doing any good; they were peeling off a half-dozen cows whenever they wanted.

"Might as well dump the whole lot and ride on," Rogers said. "We ain't gonna fulfill the contract and get paid if we show up at Fort Washington with ten cows."

"They ain't gonna let us show up anywhere with even ten cows," I said.

Jameson frowned, "What do you mean by that?"

"They want the whole bag. Our horses, guns, saddles, probably our clothes. If Montés is with them, they know what we got. And we don't even know if we're going in the right direction. We may be heading straight into the desert, on the other side of the damned Mountains."

Jameson turned to Rogers, wanting him to contradict me. But he didn't. "Marcus is probably right," he said quietly.

Chan didn't say a word. He understood, but he knew he was caught in a situation completely out of his control. His only choice was to trust us.

"So, what are we going to do?" Jameson asked.

"Cut and run," Rogers said. "We make camp tonight like we always do but saddle up just before dawn and then get the hell out of here at first light. We stampede the cows in one direction, and we ride like hell in the other."

Chan finally spoke up, "What I ride?"

"With one of us."

"What I do with ol' Henry."

"Let him go."

"No want to do that. He be with me for long time."

Rogers shrugged. "You're choice. But we ain't waiting to pull him along. If he can't keep up, we cut him loose."

"I ride him," Chan said. "He keep up."

Roger nodded. "Like I said, your choice. But we ain't gonna wait for you."

"I pack pots and pans and food?"

I stepped in this time. I didn't think Chan was getting the message about what we were up against. "Pack only what you can squeeze into a saddle bag. I suggest food and water canteens only. Keep it light 'cause that's the only chance you have to keep up with us. Do you have a gun?"

Chan frowned. "No gun."

"Do you want one?"

"Don't know how to use."

I patted him on the shoulder with affection. He had little chance of keeping up with us, and I hated to imagine what the Apaches would do to him when they caught him. "You'd better make ol' Henry run," was all I could say.

The plan almost worked.

Dawn came, and we whooped and hollered and chased them cows off in a billowing cloud of dust in a dozen different directions, and we split off in another like the devil was behind us. If you have Apaches chasing you, it's damn near the same thing.

We looked back and saw about a dozen of them Indian fellows riding like mad to push that heard back together. They were having a hard time of it, just like we hoped.

But there were three of them trailing us. Not riding hard. Just loping along, keeping sight of us.

Rogers signaled for us to slow down. We weren't gonna outrun 'em, so we might as well save our horses; it was gonna be along ride.

He looked over at me and said, "Now what?"

"Keep on moving. It's gonna take a while for them fellas to reign in the herd. The three of them behind us ain't gonna attack us on their own. Maybe we can get someplace safe before they get organized again."

Rogers glanced back again. "Is that Montés riding lead?"

I swung around for a good look. I recognized the stocky body and bandanna headband. It was Montés.

"Maybe we can bargain with him," Jameson suggested.

"Doubt it. He's chosen sides. Unless we get somewhere safe, they got the upper hand."

It was my idea, so I was the one that had to do it.

We went around a bend and would be out of sight of our stalkers for a moment or two. I dismounted, pulling my rifle out of its holster, and ran up between some boulders for a view of the back trail. They were still coming. They picked up speed so as not to lose sight of us.

I waited until they were in range. One shot. Montés fell off his horse. The other two jumped from their horses and dove behind the rocks before I could squeeze off a second shot. These boys were good. They'd done this before.

I stayed in position a few more minutes. Their horses stood stock still, waiting. Montés remained on the ground, not moving. Silence. A hawk screeched overhead. I hurried down from the boulders and mounted to catch up to Rogers, Jamison, and Chan.

We rode through the days and exhausted our water and what little food we had and huddled at night without a campfire, frozen under our blankets, barely sleeping. And still, they came. Just the two of them. Then just one of them. And then they were gone. Or so we thought.

But the desert was still endless. We might have been riding in circles. We tried to keep track of east from west and north from south, but the sun seemed to be directly overhead from mid-morning until late afternoon.

We assumed we escaped from the Indians but were now going to die in the desert. Chan was the only one that kept us going. He caught scorpions and spiders and grasshoppers, green lizards, and more rattlesnakes and started to roast them over campfires again in the evenings as we thought we were now safe from the Indians. Jameson grumbled and bitched but ate whatever Chan came up with.

Then we found the waterhole. Just in time, too, as we had been out of water for two days now. We drank from it, thirstily, and vomited. Chan tried to boil it, but we still vomited. It was rank. Repulsive. But the only water we had.

We camped next to it, trying to decide which direction to take in the morning. Chan made a good campfire that we huddled around, nibbling on the inedibles that he came up with until we fell asleep. In the morning, our horses were gone.

"Them goddamn Indians," Jameson cursed.

"Caught up with us," Rogers said.

"Took all three horses without making a noise."

"And left ol' Henry," I said.

Jameson stared at the mule. "Not enough meat on him to eat and probably too embarrassing for even an Indian to ride."

"Wha' we do now?" Chan asked.

Rogers took off his hat to rub his forehead as if he had a headache. "Walk or fight, I guess."

I looked at the desert in front of us. "Gonna be a tough walk."

"If we stay here, we got the waterhole. If Chan can keep feeding us, we can hold out for a while. Maybe they'll get tired of waiting now that they got our horses."

"Or attack us if they get bored waiting."

"We got the water, the guns, and the rocks to hide behind. That makes it their move."

"Damn," Jameson said.

That plan didn't work out. We lost our food supply. Jameson was on the outside edge of the fire, hiding behind some small boulders on night watch. Chan woke in the middle of the night to step out of the firelight to take a piss. A dozen arrows thunked into him. He fell to the ground in the darkness with a sigh.

Jameson went berserk firing into the night in every direction around us. Rogers and I rolled out of our blankets, guns in hand, but stayed on the ground to keep out of Jameson's crazed line of fire as well as from any spare arrows that hadn't been used on Chan.

When Jameson finally stopped shooting—out of ammunition?—there was only silence. No rustling sounds in the bushes. No return fire, bullets or arrows. Chan moaned softly in the shadows.

None of the three of us were going out to fetch him. Could be a setup. Lure us out there, then jump us and fill another one of us full of arrows. Chan was just going to have to wait until morning light.

Which seemed to take a year to come. But it finally did. No trace of our attackers. Vanished. Evaporated. Melted away into the desert. How do they do that?

Chan lay on the ground ten yards away, looking like a rather fat porcupine with arrows substituting for quills. Making no more sounds.

We sat to collect ourselves. Everything was untouched, except for the ammunition that Jameson wasted shooting into the dark. Again, the Indians didn't bother to take old Henry. We were amazed that Jameson didn't shoot him while he was filling the night full of lead.

"Guess we should bury him," Rogers said, looking over at Chan.

"Hell of a place to be buried," I replied. "In the middle of nowhere."

Jameson walked over to look down at the body. "We bury him, we ain't gonna get him down very far. The ground's all rock and hard dirt. A coyote or some other critter is going to come along and dig him up soon as we leave here."

"We don't bury him, the sun's coming up, and he's gonna start rotting real quick," Rogers said.

"We could eat him," Jameson said.

Rogers and I both turned to Jamison, stunned.

"Eat him?" I could barely force the words out of my mouth.

Jameson nudged Chan with his boot. "I got news for you. He's dead, and we are now out of food. We were nearly starving now in spite of what he was feeding us and I ain't scrounging around the ground looking for spiders, ants, lizards, and rattlesnakes, and I don't think you guys are gonna do so either."

"I don't know if I could ..."

Jameson leaned close as if trying to sniff him. "We gotta make up minds real soon."

"It don't seem right to eat the cook," I said.

"I never ate Chinese before," Rogers said in a failed attempt at black humor.

"I have," I replied. "One time in 'Frisco. Noodles and all kinds of spices. Rice, too. Wasn't bad."

"We ain't got no noodles," Jameson said.

Rogers smiled in spite of himself. "I bet Chan could have come up with some spices, I mean if he was the one still alive, looking to cook one of us."

We busied ourselves extracting the arrows from his body, probably causing as much damage yanking them out as they had done going in. His pants were still around his knees, proving that he was killed while taking a piss.

"Died with his hand on his pecker," Rogers said.

"Every man's dream," I added.

Jameson snorted, "I ain't gonna eat his pecker."

"Didn't get any arrows in it."

"Don't care. Still, ain't eating it."

"We could eat ol' Henry instead," Rogers suggested.

All three of us looked over at the old mule. He was nothing but skin and bones. His ribs stuck out like slats on a barrel. He stared back at us, bleating in protest against his hobbles. I wondered if he was embarrassed because the Indians hadn't stolen him. Even raggedy-ass Indians apparently have standards.

"Ol' Henry can still carry things, you know," Jameson said. "We have Chan's pots and pans and our own bedrolls, saddles, and rifles. No point in carrying all of that while we walk around out here in the desert. Ol' Henry can carry all of that, plus what water we can take, as far as he can go. Then we eat him."

He could see that Rogers and I were still not convinced. But the three of us knew we were going to die out here, one way or the other. The Indians were gonna circle back to check on us to see if the desert got us, hoping to collect our guns, clothes, and whatever else we still had, without another fight.

"If we chop Chan up, ol' Henry can also carry the leftovers when we're done," Jamison added.

"The leftovers will last longer after we cook him," Rogers volunteered, indicating that the decision had been made. But who was gonna chop him up? Then cook the parts? Which parts? Or should we put him on a spit and roast him like a hog before chopping him up?

Jameson had the best knife. A Bowie. Sharp as a razor. But he was squeamish, much more than me, or Rogers.

"We should of talked about this while Chan ... 'fore he died. He woulda' known how to do this," Rogers said.

"Just in case we thought we were gonna eat each other?" I replied. I took off my hat to wipe the sweat from my brow. It was starting to get hot, or my mind was going to explode thinking about this. "Maybe we should just bury him, let him be."

Rogers nodded, "That would be the Christian thing to do."

"He wasn't a Christian," Jameson said.

"How do you know that?"

"Chinese are heathens. Everyone knows that. I say we chop him. Carve the meat off the bone. Just skip the hands and feet and ankles and everything above the neck."

"We gonna eat the organs?" Rogers asked.

"Well," Jameson said, musing out loud, "Everyone says the liver of the buffalo tastes really good and good for you, too. And maybe the tongue. A lot of people like cow tongue."

"I ain't gonna eat no tongue. Ain't no telling where a Chinaman put his tongue," Rogers said.

"Do you think all of that will get us across this damned desert?" I asked.

"I estimate we have two-hundred miles," Rogers said, looking out at the empty horizon. "We make twenty miles a day, it'll take us ten days. If we only make ten, it'll take us twenty days. Gonna be touch and go either way. Chan may or may not last. But we have ol' Henry as a backup."

I knew two-hundred miles was a just guess. Rogers had no idea. Nor did I or Jameson.

"So, who's gonna chop him up?" Jameson asked.

I held out my hand. "Give me the knife."

Both men looked relieved.

Jamison reluctantly handed it to me. It had an elegant feel to it. Well balanced. A knife that made you want to cut something.

They both turned away as I stepped over to Chan, not wanting to watch me carve him up. I swung around, quickly cocking my Colt revolver to shoot them both in the back before they could react.

I waited until the echo of the gunshots died out in the desert vastness. I may be a dead man breathing, but I now had some extra food and more water for myself, to help me get as far I as could go.

I rubbed ol' Henry affectionally on the neck and said, "Looks like it's you and me, old partner. I'll cook 'em, and you carry 'em."

Gambler, Gunfighter, Dentist

Leslie D. Soule

John Henry "Doc" Holliday peeked out the window just for a moment, knowing that this hotel bed was to be his deathbed, and that at the age of 36, he'd made a good run of things, living fourteen years after being diagnosed with tuberculosis.

He'd come to Glenwood Springs, Colorado, believing that the hot springs there might have a positive effect on his worsening condition.

The wind howled past his window, reminding him of tumbleweeds and the dry heat of Tombstone, Arizona. At 23, he'd left for Dallas, Texas, and the drier air, but he took to life like a man with nothing to lose, and as he lay dying, realized that what mattered in life was the people you stuck by in hard times. Sometimes, if you were lucky, those folks stuck by you, too.

One of those folks he'd found out in the wild West was a lawman named Wyatt Earp. He'd saved Wyatt's life all those years ago in Dodge City, Kansas. He'd said his goodbye to Wyatt about a week ago. Doc closed his eyes for a moment.

This hasn't at all gone the way I thought my life would, all those years ago. He caught the scent of roses, that transported him with imagination's passport, to his mother's bedside. His mother lay there, dying of consumption, a vase of roses by her bed. *She died, and I couldn't save her. But I could still help people, and so I tried to, turning all the force of my mind and ability toward study, toward trying to make the world a better place, because no matter how things might end up, wasn't it valiant to stand against the rising tide of the world's turbulence?* I thought so, and with this singular thought in mind, proceeded onward.

With a degree in dentistry, useless because the tuberculosis he suffered from caused coughing fits at inopportune times like during extractions, he turned to another profession, becoming a gambler. You could make a decent living that way, if you knew what you were doing.

But Doc Holliday was physically slim and frail, so he learned how to handle weapons expertly as a way to compensate. A gambler had to be able to protect himself, for he usually stood alone.

He consulted a number of doctors, who all predicted a short life for him—but they suggested that he go out West, for the dry heat might favor his condition. And so, our story begins.

The West was full of world-roughened men, and you had to have a toughness about you, in order to get by. So, Doc Holliday, the blue-eyed, well-dressed gentleman with his neatly-trimmed mustache, became tough, and in doing so, became a part of the Wild West itself, where untold dangers lurked.

The Bee Hive Saloon & Dance Hall,
Fort Griffin, Texas

Kate walked into the Bee Hive, peering up at the sign above. The sign featured the image of a beehive and an invitation to visitors:

Within this Hive we are alive;
Good whiskey makes us funny.
Get your horse tied, come inside,
And taste the flavor of our honey.

Kate was one of the bees of this hive, and she entered and began 'buzzing' around, first alighting at the bar, where she ordered a whiskey on the rocks. The bartender poured her a glass and handed it over.

She sipped from her glass of whiskey and looked around the saloon. Then she saw someone who caught her attention. *I wonder who that handsome fellow is.*

Doc looked up as he shuffled the cards.

Kate was there to ply her trade, and she was the prime article, meaning the most beautiful woman in the room, a stunner. She made her way toward him but didn't give this goal her full attention. After all, there were plenty of potential patrons to check in with while she headed in his direction.

Eventually, Kate worked the back room, flirting with the men at the gaming tables. The West had a number of "soiled doves," that respectable society had failed. Kate's wild heart warmed to that tempest called the American West, that led so many hearts and bodies astray. She was independent but loved to flirt, and this fellow looked like he might know how to show a girl a good time.

"Hey there, handsome ... you come here often?" she said to the newcomer.

He finished shuffling the cards and set them into neat stacks. Then he folded his hands and fixed her with a blue-eyed gaze. "I'm in town for a while, but I come and go like the wind."

Don't we all.

So began the tempestuous relationship between Doc and Kate. But it's so hard to build a life on the shifting sands of time, and relationships of any kind are on high alert when the threat of impending doom looms nigh on the horizon. And yet, though you cannot control a person's ridiculous actions or their wild heart, sometimes no more can you control your own heart that beats in their direction.

It was the Bee Hive in Fort Griffin, where Doc Holliday met Wyatt Earp, as well, all those years ago. His memory transported him instantly.

Doc Holliday sat at the table shuffling cards. "Please sit. Let us talk." Wyatt pulled up a seat.

"Would you like a drink of whiskey?" Doc asked. *Just because this man Wyatt's a lawman, doesn't mean I can't afford him hospitality.* Best not to get on the bad side of the law, whenever possible.

Wyatt shook his head. "No, thank you."

"Well, I'll have one." Doc poured himself a shot. *No sense in letting good whiskey go to waste.* The strong liquor seemed to help placate the demons that eternally resided in his throat. He drank down the shot and waited for it to work its fiery magic.

"I'm looking for a man named Dave Rudabaugh and his crew. Have you heard of him?"

"I've seen him around–left town a couple days ago and it sounded like he was headed out to Kansas." Doc smiled, his blue eyes shining. "See, word's gotten around that you were trailing the gang into Texas, so I think they figured heading for Kansas would throw you off the trail."

For a lawman, Wyatt Earp seemed personable enough–a good sort of fellow, unlike all the rest of the dirty lot of vagrants that populated the West. Doc warmed to him quickly.

Wyatt Earp thanked Doc and headed to the telegraph office. At least, that's how the story went, and that's how that other famous lawman–that fellow Bat Masterson, got involved. Wyatt liked Bat Masterson, and so Doc tolerated him, and in the West, you had to tolerate people a little more than you'd do in the midst of polite society, where normally it was passive-aggressiveness that ruled. When guns were involved, a bit of caution was called for.

At any rate, that telegram went through, and then Bat—for all Doc disliked him, he had some sense—created a posse to track down Dirty Dave. He got the credit for tracking down and bringing in Dave, without realizing that he was in Doc's debt for alerting Wyatt. The outlaws were spirited away by train, out East to await a trial date.

There were outlaws, and there were scoundrels, and the thing that separated the two came down to loyalty—Doc's was unwavering. Scoundrels knew no loyalty—like one of Bat's posse men, John Joshua Webb. The story was that Dirty Dave ratted out the rest of his posse, and cut a deal to go free.

These memories streamed into his consciousness in bits and pieces. That Dirty Dave had been a scoundrel, and in the end, his head was paraded around town like it was the Middle Ages, all over again. That's the end that awaited scoundrels.

Wyatt Earp left Fort Griffin, while Doc stayed behind, and that led to a fateful brush with trouble. One day, he found himself playing cards with a man by the name of Ed Bailey. A man who was brazen and unrefined, of a rough sort of man who ran around the Wild West with no filter or inhibitions to keep his mouth or actions in check. These bullying men just ran around doing whatever the hell they wanted—and it ran in stark contrast to Doc's more refined nature.

At any rate, Doc dealt the cards, and Ed Bailey kept picking up cards off the discard pile and looking at them. This was strictly against the rules of poker.

Doc did not take kindly to Ed Bailey monkeying with the deadwood. "Come on ... cut that out," he warned, hand running down the length of one of his holstered six-shooters. But true to his brutish nature, Ed Bailey respected no boundaries. Although toying with the discard pile equaled a forfeiture of one's hand, Ed Bailey stood determined to both cheat and win. "Come on," Doc repeated. "We're here to play a fair game." And still, Ed Bailey looked at the discard pile. *Perhaps he needs a more visual sort of cue.* Doc Holliday raked in the pot with bare hands. *There, that ought to show him.*

Doc noted the flash of anger on Ed Bailey's face and saw the flash of metal as the man reached for his gun. Doc knew a thing or two about fighting. Quick as a flash, Doc's knife was in his hand, and his adrenaline was pumping. He didn't have time to bring the knife any higher than the height of the tabletop, and he tore an angry gash across Ed Bailey's stomach. The man fell onto the table, blood spilling out all over the cards.

Although Kate and the other saloon patrons explained to the lawmen who arrived, that Doc Holliday had merely acted out of self-defense, there still would need to be a trial.

"We're still going to have to take him in until a trial date can be scheduled. We're arresting him for illegal gaming until we can figure out what's going on here."

Fort Griffin did not have a jail, so Doc was kept in a hotel room until the judge could be found.

But in the Wild West, solutions could be easily found in regards to the stifling bureaucracy that threatened to take hold. But Ed Bailey had terribly dangerous friends, and they approached the hotel en masse, holding lengths of rope, for they would see Doc Holliday hanged before allowing the law to mete out justice.

The lynch mob was a gang of vigilantes known as the Tin Hat Brigade.

But as Kate was only a witness to what others saw, and a woman, besides, she was generally left alone, and thus, free to listen and move about, unnoticed.

Doc had the good sense to leave both of his six-shooters there on the table. Kate made sure to spirit them away before the arrival of the lawmen.

Kate knew she had to think fast. Either the mob or the law was bound to get to Doc and take things too far. She'd seen an old shed out back, filled with hay. All it would take was a tiny bit of fire, to create the diversion she needed, to free Doc from his hotel room. Once she had the fire going, she ran into the hotel, shouting "Fire!" and then made her way toward Doc's room.

Kate ran through the chaos, up to the second floor, and to Doc's room. She wondered how they could not be evacuating him, with the fire so close by, and growing larger by the moment. Kate removed both six-shooters from her leather satchel and pointed them straight at the guard. "Go along now, get outta here," she snarled, and the terrified guard looked only too pleased to comply. "We've got to get out of here," said Kate as she burst into the room to find Doc lying on the bed, reading.

At any rate, they rode off together to Dodge City, on the horses that Kate had commandeered. When they arrived at Deacon Cox's boarding house, Doc signed them in as Dr. and Mrs. J.H. Holliday. No one would know them here, to know the difference. For a while, Doc tried to give up gambling as a profession and go back to dentistry, thanking his lucky stars and not tempting fate further.

Likewise, Kate vowed to give up prostitution, being a dance hall girl, and frequenting saloons. For a while, there was peace in Doc's life–but it was doomed to be fleeting, and as for Kate–you could take a girl out of the saloon, but you couldn't take the saloon out of the girl. Kate had been calling herself Mrs. John H. Holliday and her shenanigans were a terrible blow to his pride.

That all being said, Doc Holliday was a man with nothing to lose–after all, all men were doomed to die–all of us who come into this world, come in knowing that someday, we are going to die. That was the price of living, the pact we made with the Creator.

In Doc's case, the Creator had merely spun those clock hands a little faster, is all. *Oh well. All men had to die sooner or later.*

Long Branch Saloon, Dodge City, Kansas

Doc Holliday sat gambling in the Long Branch Saloon. A group of cowboys rushed the town, galloping down Front Street, guns blazing, destroying shop windows. They entered the saloon and began harassing patrons. Wyatt Earp walked in the door, and several gun barrels awaited him.

Ed Morrison sneered, "Pray and jerk your gun! Your time has come, Earp!" Suddenly, there came a voice from behind Morrison.

"No, friend, you draw–or throw your hands up!" Doc Holliday had entered the fray, pointing his revolver to Ed Morrison's temple. "Any of you bastards pulls a gun, and your leader here loses what's left of his brains!" The cowboys dropped their arms.

Having relieved Tobe Driskill and Ed Morrison of their firearms, Wyatt Earp ushered them to the Dodge City jail.

Doc and Wyatt had a moment to talk.

"I'm gonna die in a gunfight, or strung up like a criminal at the gallows," said Doc. "At any rate, I'm gonna die with my boots on, like the rest of these men of the West." They walked past the Boot Hill cemetery. Doc pointed to one of the graves, where a bunch of daisies grew. "If any man tries to shoot me, Wyatt, he's a dead man ... a daisy ... I will put him in his grave." And Doc Holliday had been responsible already for the deaths of over thirty men, according to the stories about him. He shook his head. If they only knew the truth.

Tombstone, Cochise County, Arizona

Doc overhead Wyatt talking about him.

Wyatt Earp pointed toward Doc. "See that fella over there? Goes by the name o' Doc Holliday, and although he sometimes drinks three quarts of whiskey a day, he's the most skillful gambler and the nerviest, fastest, deadliest man with a six-gun I've ever seen."

Doc had to admit to himself, he'd done well at that famous gunfight, all those years ago. But it had only been thirty seconds long–and his memory of the event was sketchy at best.

Gunfight at the O.K. Corral

The shootout was between the Cowboys—Billy Claiborne, Ike and Billy Clanton, Tom and Frank McLaury on one side, and the town Marshall, Virgil Earp, Morgan Earp, Wyatt Earp, and Doc Holliday on the other side.

Frank McLaury shouted, "I've got you now!"

Doc yelled right back, "Blaze away! You're a daisy if you have!"

Morgan turned and fell. Then he saw Frank and Doc, and shot Frank McLaury in the head. At that instant, Frank McLaury's gun flashed and Doc

Holliday was shot in the hip, which fortunately for Doc, was a superficial graze.

Tom and Frank McLaury and Billy Clanton were killed. Ike Clanton subsequently filed murder charges against the Earps and Doc Holliday. The lawmen were eventually exonerated by a local justice of the peace after a thirty-day preliminary hearing and then by a local grand jury.

Then, the hearing regarding the shootout happened.

Jailer William Soule testified. William Soule, jailer and deputy sheriff, swore that the rifles were in their scabbards on Frank McLowery's and Billy Clanton's horses, "When I took them to Dunbar's livery stable."

A man pointed to the jailer, saying, "Those thrice-damned Soules are bad news, you hear? You stay the hell away from them if you know what's good for ya."

But Doc certainly didn't see any danger from this Soule fellow—the fiercest man in the West was still no match for a six-gun.

The hearing proceeded—Doc barely remembered the details these days, only the fear that gripped his heart, of the possibility of imprisonment.

In the end, Justice Wells Spicer said. "In view of these controversies between Wyatt Earp and Isaac Clanton and Thomas McLaury, and in further view of this quarrel the night before between Isaac Clanton and J. H. Holliday, I am of the opinion that the defendant, Virgil Earp, as chief of police, subsequently calling upon Wyatt Earp, and J. H. Holliday to assist him in arresting and disarming the Clantons and McLaurys ... committed an injudicious and censurable act, and although in this he acted incautiously and without due circumspection, yet when we consider the condition of affairs incidental to a frontier country ..."

And so, to Doc's relief, Justice Spicer ruled that no laws were broken in Tombstone, Arizona. The memories faded into a white-noise buzz in his brain.

Kate walked in from the other room. Doc lay dying. As it turned out, the hot springs were not the thing to cure Doc's case of consumption.

He'd asked her to be by his side at the end, the way they could have lived if life were more of a dream and less a nightmare struggle fest, and to her credit, she did come, and stay by his side until the end, and Doc Holliday died with his boots off, as though to tell him he was no outlaw, after all.

Ghost of the Vulture Mine

E. W. Farnsworth

My name is Ben Dauber. I am a newspaperman of the Arizona Territory. I want to tell the marvelous tale of how a ghost turned a man's greed into a priceless relationship with a woman. Jake Skillings was the man, and the story he told me did not have a propitious beginning. In fact, Jake's initial vision of swinging corpses promised anything but the hope of a happy ending.

Eight lifeless bodies hung from the spreading oak tree outside the Vulture Mine. Black carrion birds lined the tree's boughs, and swarms of flies rose and fell on the carcasses as the hot wind blew. Deep underground the miners plied their trade.

At the end of each day, the miners rose from the depths to find the stench of grisly remains a reminder of the penalty for stealing the smallest part of the bonanza. The foreman stood guard by the fence that enclosed the mine's entrance. Each miner leaving the mine was subject to a full body search at the whim of the foreman.

"You there. Stop and strip." The foreman had pointed to the man with his Henry rifle.

The grizzled, bearded miner did as he was told. After he stripped, he stood naked in the sunshine while one of the foreman's searchers went through his filthy clothes.

"There's nothing here," said the searcher holding up the man's clothes.

The foreman might not have heard. Then he gestured to give the miner his clothes.

Every tenth or twelfth miner had his clothing searched. The foreman kept count as the miners emerged. Only when every miner who had gone down the shaft came up again was the workday considered over.

As the last miners wandered to the berthing shacks, the foreman closed the iron door to the mine and fastened it with chains and a padlock. Now no one could enter the mine until it was opened the next morning. If anyone had remained in the cavity, he would not be able to get out.

Night fell like a curtain on the Sonora Desert. The clear skies became a black felt frame for billions of stars. Passersby with torches might make out crows sleeping in the boughs and the ropes suspending below them with the bodies.

Jake Skillings was such an unlikely passerby that evening. Young Bill Sykes was with him for the tour.

"See how those eight men serve as an example to anyone who thinks of thieving."

"Chills run up and down my spine just looking at those corpses."

Jake laughed and spat. "Summon your courage. It's going to be a long night."

"Are you sure the gold ore has been hidden where we were told?"

"There's only one way to find out. Careful. Rattlers come out in the cool darkness. You won't want to lose your share to a snakebite."

"I've got my shovel. I'm ready to dig. Just show me where."

"We've only got a few more yards to walk." Jake indicated the direction with his torch. Sparks from the torch flew into the air.

When they reached the place, Jake stopped and held the torch low to the ground to find the triangle of rocks that marked the spot.

"There are the rocks. Put your spade in the middle and start digging. I'll keep my torch over the place. Dig fast. The sooner we reach the gold, the sooner we'll load up and get out of here."

Bill dug as fast as he could. His spade hit ore almost immediately. He knelt and used his hands to uncover the pink quartz with beads of gold.

"Jake, you can see the gold."

"Don't waste time. Fill this sack."

Bill put the ore in the sack, piece by piece. When the sack was full, Jake tossed down the second sack. The torchlight was abating.

"Hurry. We won't have light much longer. The torch is going out."

"I've almost filled the second sack. Now, what should we do?"

"I'm going to tie off the first sack. Take this rope. When you're done loading the second sack, tie it off. Brush over the traces of your digging. Then follow me."

Bill took care to fill in the hole where the ore had been hidden. He lifted the heavy sack and thought he saw Jake's silhouette moving away. He followed, stumbling under his load.

Bill's mind was full of visions. He was excited about what his share of the gold would buy. Greed kept his boots moving away from the mine.

Bill whispered, "Jake, will you slow down? I can hardly see you?

Jake seemed to be going faster, not slower. He did not answer when Bill panicked.

"Jake, you've got to slow down. Please."

The silhouette disappeared in the darkness. Bill stopped to listen for the sounds of Jake's footsteps. There were no sounds. He shrugged and set his sack of gold on the ground.

Far off, a coyote howled.

"Jake, if you can hear me, tell me where you are. I think I'm lost. I don't know where we put the horses."

Bill decided to press forward in the same direction he had taken. He hoisted his sack and spade. He stumbled forward. The coyote was joined by others howling. Bill watched the stars whirling in the heavens. He tripped in a shallow hole. He was afraid it was the remains of his digging. Had he circled back where he began?

He forced himself to walk into the darkness. He lurched into a hanging figure, which swung back and forward. Bill smelled the stench. He had reached the hanging tree near the entrance of the mine. He backed into another body. As he turned, a hanging man's boots struck his hat off. He heard the beating of wings overhead.

Bill was terrified now. He knelt on one knee to get his bearings. The hanging corpses he had struck swung back and forth. A man with a torch was approaching.

"Who goes there?" the man with the torch called out.

"Who wants to know?" Jake's hoarse voice replied.

"The night watchman. Stand where you are and raise your hands."

Bill heard Jake's boots running.

"Halt. I'll shoot." Bill heard the watchman pull back his trigger and fire into the night.

A second shot replied to the first. The watchman staggered and fell. Other men were coming from many directions. Bill abandoned his sack and spade. He ran as fast as his feet would carry him. He wanted to be as far from the mine's entrance as possible. He wanted to follow Jake, but he could not hear his footsteps.

Torches were lighted on all sides. Bill could hear pistols being cocked. He raised his hands and said, "Don't shoot!"

"Stay right where you are," a booming voice rang out.

Bill did as he was told.

Three men surrounded him, each with a torch in one hand and cocked gun in the other. Bill saw that one of the three men was left handed.

"Who are you? What are you doing here?"

"My name is Bill Sykes. I'm lost."

"You have that right, son. Keep your hands in the air."

The left-handed man took Bill's gun and tied his hands behind his back.

"Hey, Max," another voice said, "Look what I found. It's a whole sack of rich ore and a spade."

The man called Max marched Bill toward the voice. Bill saw a young man looking into the sack he had filled with ore. In the torchlight, the ore glistened and gleamed.

"It sure looks like Vulture bonanza ore to me," the young man said.

Max said, "I guess we caught the man who dug it up. But where did he dig? And how did the ore get to the surface?"

"Why don't you ask him, Max?" the young man said.

Two shots rang out in quick succession. Max's body hit the ground. Then the young man slouched forward. Their torches hit the ground but did not extinguish. Bill felt a knife slicing his constraints. He heard a whisper in his ear.

"Tie up the sack of ore. Pick it up. Pick up the spade as well. Follow me, only this time don't get lost. Take this tether in your left hand. If the others catch us, I'm going to shoot you and take your share." Jake was whispering, but his voice was urgent.

Bill held the sack in his right hand and the tether in his left. Jake pulled him forward away from the dozen torches that were coming from the mining camp.

Jake's pace was relentless. The man knew exactly where he was heading. Soon they reached their horses, still tied to a giant saguaro. Jake tied together the ropes of the two sacks of ore. He slung the load over his horse's body and mounted.

Jake saw the miners were converging on their position.

"We'll have to ride in opposite directions. We'll meet at the usual place."

"I'm not leaving the gold."

"Bill, you've made the wrong choice."

Jake shot Bill through the heart. Bill dropped in the sand as his horse galloped into the darkness.

Jake saw the torches coming toward him. He fired his pistol at the closest torch bearers and earned a volley of return fire. He slumped in his saddle as he was hit and bleeding. He managed to wheel his horse and ride away from his pursuers.

Jake rode into the night, bleeding through his shirt front. He thought he was going to die, but he kept riding. Soon he heard no more shouting. Jake turned and saw no torches following him. He reined his horse and slipped to the ground. Digging a shallow hole, he buried the two bags for safekeeping near a large cholla cactus.

The next morning he rode up to a ranch just off the main trail. He passed out near the front porch.

At noon, Jake Skillings awakened lying in a bed. A woman was cleaning blood from his chest. When he tried to rise, the woman shook her head and pressed him back down.

"You're going nowhere. I've sent my son for the nearest doctor. He'll be here before mid-afternoon. You're going to have to drink water. You've lost a lot of blood."

She gave him a cup of water and pressed a poultice against his wound.

"The bullet that hit you went through your ribs. I can feel where it's sitting just under your skin in the back. You were lucky. Do you care to tell me how this happened?"

Jake nodded. "I happened across a couple of outlaws burying something just off the trail. We got into a gun battle. I got hit. My horse wandered here."

The woman shook her head. "One day, civilization will come to the Territory, but it won't come soon enough for me. My name is Regina Flowers. You're on the Flowers Ranch. What's your name?"

"I'm Jake Skillings. I'm pleased to meet you. I reckon I owe you for saving my life."

"You're not saved yet. If you can, sleep till the doctor comes."

"Thanks. I will." Jake dozed off.

It was late afternoon when Doc Kramer rode up with his kit. He examined Jake and, after using a flame on his blade, cut the bullet out of Jake's back. Regina paid him and gave him water before he hurried off to see another patient.

"I owe you for paying the doctor," Jake said. "I'll be good for it."

Regina shrugged. "If you have the means, I'll accept your repayment. Till then, your getting well is all that matters. Dinner is at sundown. Breakfast is at sunrise. Lunch is at high noon. Till you're ready to ride, you'll stay with us."

"That's mighty friendly of you. I appreciate it."

Jake stayed at the Flowers Ranch for a week before he felt well enough to help Regina's sons do light chores. He felt well enough in two weeks to ride. Meanwhile, Regina heard rumors of two men robbing the Venture Mine. One was killed and hung on the hanging tree outside the mine. The other escaped on horseback.

"Maybe this explains the men you discovered burying something along the trail."

"You may just have something there, Regina. Why, I'll bet what they were burying was the stolen gold."

"In that case, you might find it and restore it to the mine. They'd probably give you a rich reward for the gesture."

Jake smiled weakly. He knew it was more likely he would join his unlucky partner on the hanging tree. Still, he thought he should not dig up the ore right away and convey it to the assayer's office. The Vulture Mine foreman likely had warned all officials to be on the lookout for suspicious ores.

Just the same, Jake rode out to be sure he could find his hoard. He discovered it was just where he had buried it near the biggest cholla cactus patch between the Flowers Ranch and the Vulture Mine. He fetched out a large sample of the ore with beads of gold bleeding out of the roseate quartz. He reburied his sacks and brushed over all indications of his treasure trove's location.

When he rode back to the ranch, he told Regina, "I've recovered enough to be traveling. I want you to know I'll be back to repay you for your kindness."

Jake rode all the way to Phoenix to turn in his sample of ore. The assayer's eyes widened when he saw the quality of the sample, but he paid top dollar with no questions asked. After all, he had paid good money for similar samples to the German who had struck a secret bonanza. Now like the German, Jake became the target of claim jumpers who followed him whenever he left town.

It did not take him long to run through most of the money he received for the gold. He prudently kept enough to repay Regina. When he left Phoenix, he headed straight for her ranch.

"I told you I'd be back to repay you," Jake said. He handed her the cash.

"Thank you, Jake. We're even. If you need help finding that cache of gold ore those robbers were hiding when you surprised them, my boys will be ready."

"Regina, I'm not sure I even know where I was at the time. Anyhow, I'm off. If we don't see one another again, good luck to you and yours."

Jake rode directly toward his stash. He noticed two claim jumpers were following him, so he made a fire and waited for the men to close on him. The men pretended they were lost and seeking directions.

"Say, Mister, do you know the way to the Vulture Mine?"

"You're on the right road. Just keep on the trail heading west. You can't miss it. Are you looking for mining jobs? I know the foreman there is always looking for new hands."

The men looked at each other.

"No. We're looking for our own bonanza. We figure if one mine shows promise, other bonanzas must not be far away."

"You might be onto something there, but you have to watch out for jumping someone else's claim. That's a hanging matter whether you know the claim is someone else's or not."

"I'll bet you know all about that, Mister."

"I'm not sure I understand your meaning." Jake's hand went to rest just above the handle of his gun.

"Whoa, Mister. Sam meant no harm." When Jake did not take his hand away from his gun, the two men bid him adieu and rode into the sunset.

Late that night, the men returned to murder Jake and steal whatever goods and gold he had in his saddlebags.

Jake had, as a precaution, moved away from his fire. When the two robbers returned, he was hiding behind a mesquite tree.

"Howdy, boys," he said as he came from behind the tree. The men wheeled to fire, but Jake shot them both dead. He harvested their weapons, horses, gold coins, cash, and tack. It took him three hours to bury the bodies. By sunup, he was ready to unearth his treasure and reap a second sample of ore. He rode east toward Phoenix with the two horses.

In the city, Jake sold the two horses with their tack to the livery stable. He sold the weapons and ammunition to a gunsmith. He received cash for the ore. As before, he was the target of opportunists, who plotted against him in small groups.

This time Jake was careful to watch his back as he rode out of Phoenix. He often circled back on his track to catch anyone who might be following. Three men were tracking him. He turned the tables, and the hunted became the hunter. That evening, he approached them making their fire.

"Howdy, gents. Don't even try to reach for your guns. Just drop them on the ground and step back."

"We thought we'd help you harvest your gold," their leader said.

"I don't require your help, thanks. I'm going to lighten your loads." He tied the men's hands and feet and left them by the fire. He took their horses, tack, guns, ammunition, coins, and cash. He did not return to Phoenix but rode along the creek leading to the north hills. It took a week, but he rode into Flagstaff and sold the horses and hardware. In the hotel there, he thought through his situation.

Jake reasoned he was making as much robbing the outlaws who intended to prey on him as he did selling the gold ore he had stolen from the Vulture Mine. As long as he kept the myth of his private bonanza alive, he might never lack suckers to rob.

Jake decided to try out his new business plan by taking another sample from his hoard to Phoenix. By now, the three men whose horses and guns he had taken, had returned to town with a wild story of having been robbed by a ghost. Jake was pleased since his exploits now had supernatural assistance. He knew the three men would not be fooled by their own stories, so he when he left town, he lay in wait for them to pursue him.

Once again, he got the drop on the three around their campfire. A second time, he bound them hand and foot, only this time he shot each man in the back of the head. After he visited his hoard, he rode north to Flagstaff to sell his pelf and ore. On his next trip to Phoenix, he learned the ghost had killed the three men who had first reported its presence.

This time, Jake left Phoenix with no one following him. He wondered whether he had lost his charm. On the trail to the Vulture Mine, he built a fire and enjoyed the desert night. A lone rider walked his horse to the fire.

"Hello, Jake. Remember me?"

"Hi, Billy. Long time, no see."

"After you shot me dead, the mine foreman hanged me on that old oak tree. My body is still hanging from that tree."

"Are you Billy's ghost?"

"Would you believe that I am?"

"Am I awake or dreaming?"

"You tell me, Jake."

"When I pinch myself, I seem to be awake."

"That was a pretty good trick you had going. You killed and robbed the men who aimed to steal our ore."

Jake smiled. His hand reached for the area above his gun.

"That gun won't do you any good, Jake. You can't kill me twice."

Jake reached for his gun and aimed it at the ghost. He emptied it at the apparition, which laughed heartily. It was not scathed.

"Jake, you damned fool! Don't you want to know why I'm here?"

"All right, Billy. Why are you here? It can't be for the gold."

"We ghosts have no need for gold, Jake. You're right. I'm here to settle our score."

"I don't suppose I can give you anything to dissuade you from your intention?"

"I've been patient, Jake. Now I'm going to have some fun watching you try to get out of the trap I've set for you."

"Trap? What do you mean?"

"Do you think you had such success killing and robbing numerous, desperate men without supernatural help? Do you think you were just lucky to have survived your gunshot wound at the ranch where you recuperated?"

"So, you're taking credit for my successes. That's rich. You can't prove a thing."

"You're so right. Jake, I'm glad you aren't a believer. The less you believe, the better I'm going to enjoy your downfall."

Jake watched the apparition disappear. Then he was left alone in the cold desert night. He wondered whether he had been asleep the whole time of the ghost's appearance, or not.

In the morning, Jake went to the cholla cactus and dug for his sacks of ore. They were not where he had buried them.

Jake called out, "Billy, where did you hide the gold ore?"

A jackrabbit hopped out of the scrub. A herd of javelinas ran through the chollas. A roadrunner darted after a lizard. Finally, a sidewinder slithered sideways through the sand. Jake, desperate to find the rest of the ore, dug deeper, but it was no use.

Jake decided to ride to the Vulture Mine and the place where he had Billy had originally found the ore samples they had stolen. The foreman was busy lecturing the guards at the entry to the mine.

"I don't care how much you trust a man; gold will transform him. I know our miners are stealing some of our most valuable ore. They're hiding it somewhere nearby. Someone else is coming at night to take the ore away. I want you to find out who is thieving and string him up on the old oak tree beside the other claim jumpers."

Jake passed by the mine just when the foreman mentioned the claim jumpers. He looked sick.

"You. Halt. I want to talk with you." The foreman came over to Jake.

"What is your name?"

"Jake Skillings."

"Why are you skulking around so guilty-like?"

"Do I look guilty? I have nothing to fear."

"Well, if you have no business at the mine, stay well clear of it. If I find you around here again, I'll hang you from that oak tree. Do you see where those bodies are hanging? Do you see those carrion birds feasting on them? Well, you'll be just fresh meat on that tree."

Jake continued on his way, careful not to look the foreman in the eyes for fear the man would follow through on his threat without a second's thought.

Eyeing the three stones where the gold ore was hidden, he resolved to return after dark to harvest more samples. He camped two miles beyond the mine and built a fire. In the flames, he thought he saw Billy's ghost laughing at him.

That night Jake snuck back to the place where the three stones lay. With his hands, he dug fast like an animal. Two feet below the surface, he found ore samples. He placed as many as he could in a sack. He tied the sack closed with a rope and slung it over his back. Just as he was prepared to depart, he heard a voice.

"Wait. Who goes there?"

A watchman with a torch walked up, cocking his Henry rifle and looking mean.

"What have you got in that sack?"

"Why don't you have a peek?"

The man held his torch high and saw the gleam of gold. He was so struck by the luster, Jake hit him in the jaw and grabbed his rifle. He shot the man in the head. He closed the mouth of the sack and slung it over his back. He did not leave the rifle behind. When the torches came after him, he turned and fired at each of them. Though he did not hit any men, he did scare them. In the darkness, he heard their gabble when they found the murdered guard. Their excitement increased when they found where Jake had excavated to find the gold ore.

The men with torches began scrambling to harvest the gold specimens. They shot each other. In the confusion, the miners understood only their greed and the presence of the ore. The foreman's voice was rising above the others.

"If I find anyone with samples of ore above ground, I'll hang him from the oak tree. No exceptions will be made."

"I'm not giving up my gold for any man," cried one of the miners. The other men with torches repeated this mantra, punctuating their cries with shots from guns and rifles.

Jake eased away from the melee. He let the foreman and his miners fight over the gold ore. He thought he might break free entirely, but the voice of Billy Sykes cried out, "The ringleader of the thieves is over here." Right away, the torches headed for the sound of that voice. Jake made it to his horse and swung into his saddle. He rode into the night.

Jake did not stop riding until he reached the Flowers Ranch the next morning. Regina was working in her front yard when he arrived. He dismounted, and she invited him inside for coffee.

"You're looking well, Jake Shillings."

"And you're a sight for sore eyes, Regina. You haven't changed since I last saw you."

"Are you passing through, or can you stay for a while?" she asked.

"I don't want to be an imposition."

"You'll never guess what my boys found along the road to the Vulture Mine."

"What's that, Regina?"

"They found buried near a cholla cactus forest two cloth bags full of rich gold ore. Do you think the ore could have been the same those outlaws buried before they shot you?"

"It's hard to say. What have your boys done with the ore?"

"We buried the ore back of the barn. I was going to give the samples back to the Vulture Mine, but the boys convinced me there was no easy way to do that. The mine was likely to accuse us of being the robbers. We might have been hanged on that oak tree they have."

"That's good thinking, Regina."

"I so wanted to return the ore to its rightful owner. I guess things aren't simple under the law."

"I think your boys found the ore, so it's their property. They didn't steal it. They brought it home. Now that it's on your land, it's yours."

"I'm not entirely satisfied with that arrangement, but it will have to do."

"I've heard the security at the mine is thorough. I don't know how those outlaws managed to steal any samples. Why, the foreman searches the miners every day at the close of business. Some miners must be taking extraordinary risks to keep their theft secret from the foreman."

"How do you know so much about mine security?"

"It just stands to reason a mine would take precautions."

Regina poured him coffee and offered a crust of bread with honey from the wild honeybee hives she kept at the back of her property.

"No one has been nosing around asking about the ore, has he?"

"If anyone's been doing that, he's not been asking here."

"I think you can rest easy about the ore as long as you don't try to sell it to an assayer."

"I suppose you know how to do that?"

"When you need money, just let me know. I have a friend in the Phoenix assayer's office. I can get you top dollar for your ore. With me as your agent, you won't be identified as having anything to do with the ore. I'll be willing to take the risk at no cost to you."

"I don't want you to take risks without being rewarded for it."

"Would it be fair to ask for ten percent of the assayed value of the ore plus a small fee for transportation?"

Regina and Jake shook hands on those terms. She had an immediate need for cash to buy forty acres of an adjacent ranch. Jake helped her dig up the sacks of ore. He put two samples in his saddlebags before they reburied the rest in the back of the barn. Jake rode off for Phoenix. He got top dollar for her samples and returned with the cash.

Once again, he became the target of outlaws who wanted to jump his bonanza claim. He outsmarted his pursuers as he always did. When he showed up at the Flowers Ranch, he had not only the cash, net his expenses, but also four horses, tack, six shooters, ammunition and two rifles.

Regina was delighted at this turn of events. From Jake's deals, her sons each received two mounts with tack, a rifle, two handguns, and ammunition. Jake taught her sons to shoot. She bought her neighbor's acreage for cash. Jake surveyed her new land with her. He congratulated her on her business acumen.

Jake remained on the Flowers Ranch for well over a month. During that interval, Regina seized other opportunities. One such was the purchase of fifteen head of cattle. Another was her purchase of a right-of-way for an irrigation canal to bring water to half of her ranch in monsoon. The irrigation was of ancient Indian manufacture. Jake worked with Regina's sons to improve the purchase so it ran life-sustaining water to their alfalfa crops and their livestock.

One day, Regina asked Jake for his advice about sheep ranching.

"Regina, you know cattle and horses. Sheep are an entirely different matter. I'd advise you to avoid sheep unless you can find a sheep rancher with experience. Then you can drive a bargain for the sheep."

An old half-Indian shepherd Regina had met agreed to tend her herd of sheep under certain conditions. She offered him a hundred acres and a dwelling if he would be her shepherd.

"Well, Jake, Manuel has agreed to my terms if I will pay him fifty gold dollars and give him a permanent lease on one hundred acres of my land."

Jake, who was a wizard at deals like this, said, "That would be a good deal for both of you. I suggest you extend the offer, so Manuel receives your acreage in the event of your death."

"What about my two sons?" she asked.

"Draw up the papers so Manuel pays your sons in cash or heads of sheep for every year he occupies your hundred acres."

"If he agrees to my terms, I'll have to sell the rest of my gold ore."

Jake thought that over. "Regina, I'll convert your gold ore to cash, but your reserves will then be gone. You'll have to deal with the consequences by other means. Do you want me to proceed?"

When Regina told Jake to get her the money for the gold ore, they excavated the ore. Jake had to use a wagon to take the ore to the assayer in Phoenix, who was delighted to give him top dollar for his bonanza ore. Jake had the foresight to take Regina's two sons along for the trip. On their return, they had the usual company of outlaws looking for easy pickings.

The first night out of Phoenix, Jake told the boys to lounge around the fire while he provided overwatch for them. Four bandits tried their luck at poaching, but Jake killed all four. Behind the wagon on tethers were four dead men's horses with tack. The wagon held the arms and ammunition of the bandits. Jake and the boys buried the malefactors in the desert so they would never be found.

The second night, an even larger band of outlaws tried to rob the Flowers boys. Again, Jake killed them all. The next morning, the burials took longer than before. Once underway, the wagon was now followed by a dozen horses. The pile of weapons amounted to ten rifles, thirty guns, and ammunition for all weapons. Additionally, gold and silver coins, bills and rings made their haul worth a small fortune.

The third night, Jake prepared for a siege. He helped the boys turn the wagon on its side. He ran a string line to tether the sixteen-odd horses. He and the Flowers boys built a fire that was a decoy. Meanwhile, they took positions with fields of fire that covered the entire area without running risks of friendly fire. When the outlaws came, they were well armed and well-coordinated. The battle raged into the early morning. It took an entire day to strip the victims and fill the righted wagon with the harvested arms. Now Jake and the boys had thirty horses with full tack, forty rifles, over a hundred handguns and plenty of ammunition for their needs.

Though they made the same preparations for the fourth night, no attackers appeared. Jake and the boys spelled each other through the night. In the morning, they pressed onward to the Flowers Ranch where they corralled the horses and stowed the arms and ammunition inside their farmhouse. The amount of cash, coins, and jewels they brought home made Regina's eyes water. She asked no questions as she counted the money while stowing it in her cash box.

"Jake, you've returned with far more than I bargained for. How can I repay you?"

"You've paid me ten percent plus expenses for the negotiation of the gold ore. What more should I ask?"

"You've taken what you bargained for, but my boys have learned how to defend what they have from you. You've taught them that more must be done than barter and trade. Your contribution to their education is priceless."

That evening as Jake, Regina and the two boys digested their dinner around a roaring fire in the living room of the farmhouse, they heard a great commotion outside. Jake positioned Regina and the two boys at intervals with guns and ammunition to support a siege.

When he had briefed them what to do, he crept out the back door with his two six guns, two bandoliers with ammunition across his chest and a Bowie knife stuck in his belt. He was uncertain whether he would have supernatural assistance in this night's fight. But he resolved to take his assailants to Hell with him.

The outlaws attacked in hourly waves. Jake's presence outside completely surprised the enemy forces. As the outlaws fired toward the house, they revealed their own positions. Jack slipped back of each man who fired and slew him. He moved like a spirit. Thus he defeated each wave though, to be sure, Regina and her two sons gave withering return fire against the attackers.

Jake at one interval piled outlaws' bodies in the area in front of the farmhouse. He used flammables to make a huge funeral pyre for the bodies. He used a torch to set the pyre alight.

The blaze of bodies made the attackers visible for a mile. As the fatty parts of the bodies ignited and spat, the smells of burning human tissue served as a warning to the outlaws of what would become of any who dared come forward.

The outlaws decided to charge the farmhouse from all sides. Regina and her boys were ready. More importantly, Jake was ready to make a circuit of the attackers, killing them as he went. Every time the outlaws withdrew, Jake dragged new bodies to the pyre.

"Not bad, Jake," said the ghost of Billy Sykes.

"Whose side are you on, Billy? I'm outnumbered and outgunned just as I was the night you died."

"You chose to kill me, old friend."

"Admit you were more trouble than you were worth, my friend."

The ghost smiled and vanished.

Jake continued killing until dawn. He did not rest on his laurels but led the two Flowers boys to round up the outlaws' horses and strip the bodies of their guns, money, and ammunition. Regina counted their harvest.

"Jake, you're making me a believer in your manner of making money. I must admit, though, we'll need to dig a mass grave to accommodate all the bodies that litter my property."

Regina's boys used the horses to drag the bodies to a wash. They filled the wash with corpses. They drew a harrow over the bodies, making the ground level where the mass grave lay.

The corral was now full of horses. They had to build new corrals to redistribute the herd. Inside the farmhouse, the collection of saddles, reins and saddle blankets was enormous. Regina's cash box was bursting, so Jake had to hide sacks of cash and coins in the barn.

The advantage of their resistance was the Territory was now rid of many notorious outlaws. Regina and her sons were now veterans of self-defense. Jake had bonded with a family, of sorts, to defend what was worth defending.

Because the attacks had been outlaw attacks, the authorities took no notice. Only the assayer noticed that the quality of the gold ore sold by Jake Shillings matched nothing outside of the bonanza found at the Vulture Mine. Naturally, the assayer communicated this finding to the owners of the Vulture Mine. They took notice and began an investigation. The focus of their study quickly gravitated to Jake.

The Territorial Marshal showed up at the Flowers Ranch two weeks after the stunning defeat of the combined outlaw forces. The marshal did not come alone. He was accompanied by five deputies.

"Mrs. Flowers, I have a few questions regarding Jake Shillings. Do you have the time to answer them?"

"I'll do whatever I can to help your investigation, Marshal."

"Do you know a man named Jake Shillings?"

"Yes, Marshal, I do. He taught my sons and me the art of self-defense. We all would have died without his training."

"Do you know how Mr. Shillings made his living?"

"I only know he's the most resourceful man I've ever known. He advised me on purchases of land and livestock. He helped me out of several attempted robberies and outright murders. I'd say he makes his living by teaching survival skills."

"How did you first meet Mr. Shillings?"

"He rode onto my ranch, wounded by outlaws around two years ago. I called the doctor and nursed him back to health. After that, he returned periodically to help me in return for helping him."

"Do you have any evidence Mr. Shillings ever stole gold ore from the Vulture Mine or from any other reputable mining concern in the Territory?"

"I've never heard such slander, Marshal. I've trusted Mr. Shillings with my deepest financial secrets. He's been a father to my sons. He has risked his life on numerous occasions to protect me, my family and my possessions."

The marshal shook his head. "Thank you, Ma'am, for being candid with me. One more question, do you know where Mr. Shillings is right now? I have some questions I'd like to ask him personally."

"Well, Marshal, he left here a week ago. I can never predict when he's likely to show up again. He's always turned up when things get really bad for me. Right now, things have never been so good. I wouldn't be surprised if he stayed away for six months or a year."

"Please do him and me a favor by telling him I'm looking for him to ask a few questions. I'm not looking to accuse him of any crimes. I think, though, he might be able to help me solve a few crimes. Will you do that for me?"

"Are you asking whether I'll pass on your message about wanting to ask him questions?"

"Yes, I am."

Regina said, "I'll gladly tell him you're looking to ask him questions. Is there anything else, Marshal?"

"No, Ma'am. Have a great day." He turned to his deputies and told them, "Boys, we'll be pressing onward." He and his boys rode out to the trail leading toward the Vulture Mine. They were over the horizon when Jake climbed down from the second story of the barn.

"Well, Jake, you guessed it. The marshal wants to ask you questions."

"By the law of the land, it's time for special measures."

"Whatever do you mean, Jake?"

"Regina, you're a widow, but you're still a fine young woman as far as I can see."

"And your point is, Mr. Shillings?"

"I mean, Regina, will you marry me?"

"Why don't you come inside for a cup of coffee. I think you've opened a whole new line of inquiry. I'm inclined to say yes, but I need to know what I'm getting into. I also have to be concerned about what I'm getting my two sons into."

Regina opened their discussion with a simple question, "Is there anything I should know about your past that I don't already know?" She poured him coffee as she asked this.

He said, "Where do I begin? You know that I've killed a few men in my time."

She nodded and drank from her coffee cup. "In the Territory, a man does what he must. Are you wanted for any specific murders or crimes?"

Jake shook his head. "Not that I'm aware of. Also, I've never served time in jail or prison."

"Well, that's something. Are you going to tell me about how you got your scars?"

"If I thought those stories would help you know me, I would tell you, but I don't."

"Have you ever been married?"

"No. And I've never sired children that I know of."

Regina smiled.

"All right, Regina. I'm going to turn the questioning right back on you."

"My only husband was Ben Flowers, who died defending me, the children and this ranch. Hank and Stew are my only children. Like you, I've killed men to defend my family and property. I've never been arrested or accused of a crime. My boys likewise are free of blame. I'd like to know whether you have any strong faith in the Lord or belief in an afterlife."

"I'm not a church-going man, and I'm not fit to be on a first name basis with God. If there is an afterlife, I'm likelier to go to Hell than Heaven on account of evil thoughts I've had. I see a ghost now and then. He doesn't scare me, exactly. But he comes and threatens me."

"Do you care to elaborate on that?"

"Not unless you want me to."

"In the Sonoran Desert, at night, I've had my share of visions. I've seen the pale white horse. I've seen Apaches on the warpath. As a mother, I've had apprehensions about my sons."

"Is there anything you would want your future husband to know about you specifically?"

"I want my ranch to pass to my sons in equal parts when I die."

"If you want to make a will with that stipulated, I've no objection."

"I'd want my husband to enjoy my body as often as I'd like."

"That you wouldn't want to put in writing."

Her eyes found his and held them for a long while. When she turned to look at her hand, his hand covered hers.

"Well, Regina, if you're satisfied, I'll ask the question. Will you marry me?"

"Yes, Jake, I will marry you. I never guessed the man I nursed back to health after he was shot would be my second husband."

"We'll get married in Gilbert as soon as you like. I'll have to buy a ring. You may want to make a wedding dress. I'll have to find the wherewithal to make the purchases."

"Don't worry about that. I kept aside some ore samples for the purpose. They're hidden in the barn in a special place."

Jake and she went to the barn to fetch the ore, which may have been the richest in containing pure gold of all the samples from the two sacks of ore. After discussing what was needed, Jake made a list and rode to Phoenix to sell the ore and buy the dress that Regina described to him.

On the trail, Jake was intercepted by four hard men. They did not recognize him, but they asked him about a man who frequently carried gold ore from a bonanza to the assayer's office in Phoenix.

"Men, I believe I met the prospector you're looking for. He's average height and weight. He usually wears a broad-brimmed hat and has a two-holstered belt with six guns. Sometimes he carries a Henry rifle."

The leader of the four said, "That's the man to a T. When and where did you see him last?"

"I saw him up by the Vulture Mine around seven days ago."

The leader looked at his men. "Well, boys, let's get right up to the mine and start searching from there." He turned one last time to Jake and rested his eyes on Jake's bulging saddle bags. "Thanks, Mister. Be safe on your journey. Outlaws are everywhere in these parts. They'll kill a man, strip him and leave his carcass to the crows and vultures."

The four men rode down the trail. Jake saw how the dust from their horses showed they turned around and rode in a wide circle around him. He guessed they would ambush him sometime during the night.

Jake prudently buried his ore at the foot of a giant saguaro and marked the place with a cairn of stones. He rode away from the saguaro and built a campfire after tethering his horse. He kept his two six-shooters ready for the ambush.

In the middle of the night, Jake heard the unmistakable sounds of men approaching his fire pit.

"Who goes there? Identify yourselves, or I'll shoot."

"Hold your fire, Mister. It's just my boys and me. We met you on the trail to Phoenix this afternoon."

"Did you lose your way?"

"No. I think we found the man you described. It was you, wasn't it?"

Before Jake could answer, the voice of Billy Sykes said, "He's your man all right. Why don't you kill him and take his body to the Vulture Mine for the big reward?"

"What reward?" the leader asked.

"A reward of one thousand dollars in cash or gold has been posted for the presentation of the body of Jake Skillings, dead or alive. That's the man you see lounging by the fire."

"If that's so, why haven't you turned him in for the reward?" The leader of the four evidently did not know he was talking to a ghost. In this, Jake saw an opportunity.

"Billy, will you tell me again how you died?"

"You know that well enough, Jake. I had harvested two bags of rich ore we found buried near the mine. Everyone was shooting at us as we tried to escape. You killed me in the dark and took the ore."

"Will you now please tell me where you dug for the ore?"

"That's easily answered," Billy's ghost said. "It was in the center of the three prominent rocks near the old oak hanging tree of the mine. There's much more where those two sacks came from."

"You wouldn't spite me by taking these four men to the place they can find the rest of the ore, would you?"

"Hahaha. That I would do, just to spite you, Jake. Men, do you want to stay here and risk death at the hands of Jake Skillings or go with me to the Vulture Mine for the mother lode of hoards?"

"Show us the way to the mother lode. If we ride hard, we might arrive before morning."

Jake heard the men retreating to mount their horses. They rode into the night with the voice of Billy Sykes leading them like a will-o-the-wisp. Jake relaxed somewhat and stoked his fire. He marveled at the power of greed to steer the plans of desperate men. He had not thought much about how Billy might help him one day.

The next morning, Jake unearthed his ore samples and rode to Phoenix where he sold the ore to the assayer. He used some of the money he received to buy his wife the wedding dress she wanted. He rode to Gilbert to arrange for a preacher to perform the wedding ceremony. Finally, he bought himself a suit of clothes as befitted the groom.

When he returned to the Flowers Ranch, the two boys had been hard at work. A new sign for the Flowers-Skillings Ranch had been painted. A long picnic table had been erected for the wedding feast. Regina had baked a dozen pies. A fire pit was ready to receive the steer they intended to sacrifice for the repast.

"Jake, you probably haven't heard the news. Four men were taken near the Vulture Mine as they dug for ore. They sang a story of a ghost who led them to the place where they were digging. The foreman of the mine and ten or so miners caught them red-handed. Now they're going to hang from the old oak tree."

"I think it was greed that caused their downfall, not a ghost."

"You may be right, future husband. Anyway, I thought you might want to ride to the mine with the two boys so they can see the hanging. It will be a life-long lesson for them about the wages of sin."

"Regina, the boys have vivid imaginations. I'm sure they know what will happen when a rope chokes the life out of a man. Shouldn't you be seeing a lawyer to make your will?"

"You're right. While I'm away, why don't you and the boys ride the perimeter and mend the fence?"

Jake and Regina's two sons spent the next two days mending fence while she saw the lawyer and returned with her copy of the will.

Jake saw Regina's will left her estate to her two sons, but there was a provision allocating her estate in equal shares to all her children. This was her way to include her future children sired by Jake.

Regina put it this way, "Jake, the wording of my will is to encourage you to make every effort to sire children with me, the more, the better. That constant effort will keep me healthy and happy for the rest of my life."

On the Sunday appointed as the wedding day, Jake, Regina and the two boys hitched up the wagon. They went to the church in Gilbert for the ceremony. They returned to the Flowers-Skillings Ranch for the feast, where neighbors from ranches in the area stopped by that evening. When all the guests had departed, Jake and Regina sat in front of the fire under the stars.

"Are you happy, Regina?"

"I will be happy after we've gone to bed to consecrate our wedding."

She was, Jake found, correct. He had never seen a happier woman in his life the next morning. He felt exhilarated too. His life had new meaning because he had a quest, to sire as many children as he could with his new wife.

On his way back from the Venture Mine, the newspaper writer Ben Dauber happened to drop by the ranch to interview the nuptial pair.

"What did you see at the mine, Ben?" Regina asked.

"It was the hanging of four men on the hanging oak tree. They had an unlikely story about a ghost having led them to dig for stolen ore at a specific location. When the foreman looked into the matter, he and his men found a mother lode of high-grade ore. There was so much gold ore at the spot, a representative of the owners of the mine came to do an inventory."

Jake said, "There must be a story about how the gold ore got out of the mine and into the location where the men dug it out of the ground."

"I'm still trying to solve that mystery."

"Would you like the speculation of an amateur?" Jake asked.

"I'm open to suggestions," Ben said.

"The security of that mine is stringent to a fault. The foreman and his guards select miners at random for full-body searches every evening when the mine closes. It's therefore highly unlikely that the foreman and at least some of the guards were in on the theft from the start."

"That's not a bad theory. It could be that the foreman knew nothing about the theft. It may be the work of one or more guards and possibly one or more miners too."

"I think I know how you can sort out what you need to know for your solution—and your story."

"I'm all ears."

"Do you have time to stay on this ranch overnight and do some fire gazing with me?"

"Jake, Ben can stay, but I'm not going to let him interrupt your connubial duties." Regina was insistent, and Jake could only shrug.

"I suppose I could stay through the night."

"I'll build a fire in the fire pit. When it's time, I'll introduce you to Billy Sykes. You will find he's a reliable informant. By morning, you'll have your story."

Ben helped Jake build the fire. He situated his saddle and saddle blanket so his head would face the flames. Jake's saddle and saddle blanket lay on the ground beside Ben's gear.

At nightfall, Jake set the pyre alight. He encouraged Ben to keep the fire alive so Billy Sykes could appear whenever he liked.

Regina was ready to retire shortly after sundown. Jake went to her and closed the door for a long while. Around midnight, he emerged and joined Ben in front of the fire.

Billy Sykes came as an image in the flames when Jake called him.

"Billy Sykes, this is Ben Dauber, the newshound. He wants to know how the gold ore got out of the Vulture Mine and into the ground marked by the three stones. Will you enlighten him?"

The ghost of Billy Sykes laughed. "The mystery is easily solved. The foreman, two guards, and two miners conceived a plan for the lead of the syndicate for the owners of the mine. To capitalize, they daily extracted rich ore, which they sequestered secretly and buried outside the mine. The ore was never inventoried as part of the owners' share. Half of the value of the ore was to line the pockets of the syndicate. The other half was to be split among the foreman, who gained a fourth of the whole, and the four others, each of whom would receive a sixteenth of the whole."

Ben Dauber was furiously making notes. "The math works out! How long has this scheme been going?"

Billy's ghost said, "It's been going as long as the current foreman was appointed. He formerly worked for the syndicalist who had the idea."

"Can you prove this?" Dauber asked the ghost.

"I can let your eyes be witness to the truth. The syndicalist is coming for his share of the ore two days from now. He's afraid the discovery of the hoard will cause it to be counted with the current owners' share."

Jake said, "It seems to me that the others will be worried they won't get their shares as well."

"In fact, they are worried. One night earlier than the syndicalist's arrival, the foreman plans to take half of the ore to a secret hiding place of his own."

"I'll bet he doesn't plan to share it with his co-conspirators."

"Jake, you always did think like an arch criminal. That's why the complicit guards and miners plan to take half the ore this very night and divide it before they scatter separately."

Jake laughed out loud. "By the four complicit people acting first, they'll each get four times what they would have received from the original deal. They'll take their additional shares out of the foreman's share. He, in turn, will be getting a lesser share, but he will decimate the share expected by the syndicalist. It's a perfect Robin Hood venture."

Ben Dauber did the math again with the assumption that each faction would execute their plan. "What if the foreman were caught in the act?"

"Do you want that to happen?" Billy's ghost asked.

"I'm just a fly on the wall," the newshound said.

"Jake, what do you think?"

"Billy, how did it feel when you caused those four desperadoes to be hanged on the old oak tree?"

"I felt partially vindicated. I wasn't the only person hanging from that tree."

"Why don't you have more fun revealing the crimes of others? In fact, can you figure the maximum number of men you might get hanged for this plan?"

"Jake, you're breaking my head. But it would be fun. I'll be going now. If I hurry, I can raise the alarm as the guards and miners unearth their portion."

Billy's ghost disappeared. Ben Dauber looked at Jake with a wild surmise.

"If I'm going to write this story, I'll have to be a witness on site. I'm going to saddle up and ride for the Vulture Mine this very night."

"Maybe I'll go with you, Ben."

"I heard that, Jake. You'll do no such thing. Let your newshound friend ride for his story. I want you to get right back in here and ride for your life."

Jake shrugged at Ben. "I've work to do. Good luck with your quest. If you get the chance to stop by afterward to tell me how things went, I'd appreciate it."

Regina, dressed in her nightgown, came to lead Jake to their connubial bed. Ben rode into the darkness. The fire had become embers glowing like orange worms in the fire pit. Billy's ghost was long gone.

"So, your friend's ghost came in the night?" Regina said as she set her nightgown aside and slid into her husband's arms.

"Ben fancied he came. Anyway, both are gone."

"And here we are, husband. I plan to have you make the most of the rest of the night for both of us. As for dreams of gold, I'll make them disappear."

Jake learned that night the power of his new bride's vision. Preoccupied, he forgot the gold for the moment.

Only when I, Ben Dauber, came by a few days later did he confess he had spent the interval in his wife's loving arms. Meanwhile, the ghost had been busy too. Six men were slated for hanging now, but no one could tell where all the gold ore went.

Morgan Meade

Matthew Gowans

Morgan Meade wakes up and immediately regrets it.

The man standing over him, with a handgun resting on his thigh, could have been anyone. The sun has risen, after all, and the light in Morgan's tired eyes has made the figure above him into nothing more than that—a figure. The person looking down at him could be a woman, for all he knew. Maybe they're not even looking down at him. Maybe—and Morgan acknowledges the implausibility of this particular 'maybe'—they haven't seen him at all, and they're just enjoying the view, completely oblivious to the man with the bloody forehead lying at their feet.

But he does know who it is. And when his eyes have finally adjusted, he sighs.

"You son of a bitch," he says.

Lawrence Wildrick sighs back. "Christ, Morgan. I mean, Christ! It was only a hand!"

He'd been tracking Lawrence Wildrick for quite some time now. Three months, maybe four. Since leaving Gosset, Morgan's sole purpose on this earth had been to find the man who left his life in ruins and put him in the ground.

But right now, Morgan needed sleep.

A few hours ago, he'd spotted smoke from what he'd assumed was a campfire. Now, his assumption confirmed, he surveyed the three strangers who were perched around the flames.

The men appeared to be playing a card game of some sort. Neither seemed enthralled in what was taking place, but both were taking frequent swigs from what appeared to be a whiskey bottle, so their boredom would likely fade soon. In Morgan's experience, whiskey was more than enough to liven up a tedious game of cards.

The woman appeared to be sleeping, but from this distance, it was hard to tell for sure. To her right were two horses, and what he assumed was a wagon of some kind, he couldn't really see it behind the foliage.

Two guns lay in the dirt. They were both quite some distance from the men, so unless they had more weapons tucked beneath their shirts, neither was currently armed.

Before Wildrick came along, Morgan was quite the shooter. He was known for it, in fact. But that was some time ago. While he was confident he could take out both men without difficulty, he had just three bullets left in his gun. If the woman awakened and turned out to be armed, or the men really were hiding pistols in their shirts, or if just one of Morgan's shots went wide … his search for Wildrick would be over. He was in no way prepared to let that happen.

Still, there was also a good chance he wouldn't need to start shooting. But he simply couldn't stop the thought from entering his mind—that mind once belonged to a gunslinger, after all.

There was a time in his life when he'd have spent hours surveying these people, getting a read on them, deciding how to approach the situation— deciding if there even was a situation.

He no longer had that patience. So, with his gun in hand and his knife close by, he put two fingers in his mouth and whistled.

The men armed themselves immediately. It was a fast maneuver, and quickly they were in a standoff with the shrubbery. Morgan stayed crouched, hidden in the foliage.

The woman, while awake and on alert, stayed where she was. As Morgan had suspected, she appeared to be unarmed.

"Who's out there?" the younger of the two men yelled. "Show yourselves! Show yourselves, or we start shootin'!"

"There'll be no need for any of that tonight, good sir," Morgan replied.

"Who are you?" shouted the same man. "What d'you want?"

The woman looked over her shoulder, either at the horses or the wagon, or both. For the first time since he'd settled behind the bushes, it occurred to Morgan that there could have been more men inside that very wagon. More armed men.

Morgan took a long breath and prepared to ask the question that he'd asked a hundred times in the last few months.

"I want a word if it do ya fine. Name's Morgan Meade. I'm … I'm looking for someone."

The men exchanged a glance.

"This 'someone.' Now, who might that be?"

"He goes by Lawrence Wildrick. Sometimes Wild Rick, but not for some time now. You boys know a man by that name?"

Again, the men's eyes locked. This time, when the same man started to speak, the older one cut him off.

"We might've heard of him," he called, scratching his neck with his free hand. "Yeah. Sounds familiar. Why you … why you lookin' for him?"

There was every chance the man was lying. But why would he do that? To lure this stranger in and rob him? They had two horses and a wagon. What more could a man need? Certainly, nothing that Morgan had to offer. Unless they needed two sips of warm water and the first edition of Dan Bidder's Trail's End.

"Well," he replied. "I'll be honest …"

He paused and emerged from the shrubbery just enough so the men could see his face. And then he smiled.

"I want a word with him too. You might say we have some … unfinished business, as it were."

The younger man chuckled softly. If they were planning on robbing him, or worse, they were hiding it well.

"Didn't peg you as a ghost, Mister Meade."

Morgan nodded, before trying to chuckle himself. It had been a while since he'd done so, and it came out all wrong.

"So," he said. "Wildrick. Any idea where he might reside? What was the last thing you heard about him?"

"Ah," the older man said. Now that Morgan was closer, he could make out the patchy mustache above his upper lip. "I think we could discuss that over some whiskey, that sound good to you? What say we put down our guns and have ourselves a little chit-chat? I'm William, by the way. That there's Sam."

He failed to mention the woman's name. She didn't seem to mind.

Morgan nodded slowly. It was decision time. He wouldn't quite say he trusted the men, that if they were going to screw him over it was a bit late to do much about it now. Besides, he could certainly use the rest.

"Sounds good to me."

"Great! I am mighty pleased. We'll have a few drinks, tell ya all we've heard … hell, you can have an hour with our Agnes for all I care," William said, laughing and gesturing at the woman.

She hung her head, but before her eyes went out of view, Morgan noticed something about them that he would never have clocked way back in the shrubbery, they were extremely bloodshot. He'd only seen eyes that red one other time in his life—when he was eight, his older brother had been shot in the hand. Wyatt had been fine in the long run, aside from the finger that their father had to remove, but his mother had gotten quite the shock. And maybe Morgan was misremembering, but at the time it seemed like she was crying for several days. By that point, her eyes had been slightly less red than Agnes's were right now.

"She's quite somethin', I'll tell ya that," said William. "Quite somethin'. Ain't that right, Sam?"

Sam smiled, but he was shaking his head a little. Unlike the man on his right, he'd clearly noted the change in Morgan's face.

And that was when his eyes found the wagon. A touch more of the vehicle was in view now, and it hadn't been hiding more men—it had been hiding a cage. A cage big enough to fit a human. Specifically, Morgan assumed, a female one.

Morgan sighed.

"Sounds like a lovely evening, gentlemen," he said.

He shot at William first. The bullet went right through his forehead. In the same instant, he also shot at Sam, this bullet missed.

Morgan blinked. When he'd raised his weapon, just like every other time he'd ever raised his weapon, the mind of a gunslinger had smothered every other instinct. That mind was not used to missing. In the moment it took him to squeeze the trigger once more, Sam shot him in the arm.

Morgan cried out, and suddenly his gun was on the ground before him.

Agnes, who had been screaming since William hit the ground, turned to run.

Sam rushed toward Morgan before he could retrieve the gun. He kicked at the weapon, presumably to slide it out of Morgan's reach. It barely moved, and the man gave a yelp—guns, even the smallest ones, are heavy things—it was a wonder

Sam had forgotten this, considering one was in his hand, but he was not deterred for long. Seconds later he was throwing it toward the campfire.

"You son of a bitch," he muttered, every now and then glimpsing at the body of his friend. It was during the second glimpse that he realized Agnes was getting away. She was headed for the horses and getting very close.

Sam cursed loudly, then two bullets left his gun. Only one found its target, appeared to go right through her calf, but it was enough to bring her to the ground.

The man trundled to the horses. On the way, he took William's gun from the dead man's holster and Morgan's gun from the dirt. "You even think about tryin' something," he yelled back at Morgan. "The next one goes in her head. Y'hear me?"

Through the growing pain in his right arm, Morgan nodded.

"I'm makin' the most a' this," Sam said. "I am makin' the god damn most a' this!"

Agnes was sobbing. She was clutching her leg with both hands in a futile attempt to stop the bleeding. Moments later those hands were bound at the wrists, with the rope Sam had retrieved from the horses.

Morgan opened his eyes. He'd been drifting for a moment there, every blink getting longer than the last.

"Get in," he heard Sam yell, and Agnes returned to her mobile prison, tears flowing down her cheeks.

And then Morgan was in the wagon, and then Sam was throwing bandages at them, and then Agnes was reaching for those bandages and pulling up his sleeve.

"Y'all better be alive when we get where we're goin', I swear to god," Sam said, but the voice was far away.

Morgan reminded Agnes that she had her leg to take care of and that she should tend to her own wound first. She laughed, or at least Morgan was fairly sure she laughed, probably not, actually, considering their current situation, and then she said, "You said that ten minutes ago, dummy, and I did my leg first. You should get some sleep."

He nodded softly, murmuring in agreement—agreement with what?—and then his eyes stayed closed for three hours.

As it turned out, the bullet had gone right through Morgan's arm. Upon waking, he asked Agnes if the same could be said for her calf.

"Don't worry about it," she said, dismissing the query with a wave of her hand. "I'm fine."

There appeared to be blood seeping through her bandages. But she probably knew that, so he kept his mouth shut for a second before finally thanking her.

"If you hadn't been here, I don't quite know if I'd have ever woken up."

She laughed, or gave it her best shot, anyway. The wagon hit a bump in the road, and her voice jumped a little. At some point Sam had thrown some kind of cover over their cage, so all he could tell for sure was that the sun still wasn't up. "You'd have been fine. Seem like a tough old boy. Thanks for killing William, by the way. He was without a doubt the worse of the two."

Morgan nodded. "Seemed that way. His friend, though ... why's he kept us both alive? He said something ... before I passed out, I can't recall ..."

"Yeah. He said he was gonna 'make the most outta this,' or somethin' like that. He sorta explained it while you were asleep. Their original plan, well, William's original plan, was to go down west and sell me. They know some folks down there who would, in his words, 'greatly appreciate my company.' But when you came along and started talkin' 'bout that Lawrence, uh ..."

"Wildrick."

"Right, him ... I guess they assumed you wanted him dead. As did I."

"I wasn't exactly subtle about it," Morgan smiled.

"No, you were not. And now Sam's got a new plan. He's gonna find Lawrence Wildrick, and he's gonna sell you to him. I should mention that he also assumes since you wanna kill this guy, that this guy's gonna wanna kill you."

"It's ... complicated. So, you think he can pull that off? This Sam guy? And what happens to you in all this?"

"He said he wasn't sure what he'd do with me. He said ... he said maybe he'll keep me, after all. Without William, and again I quote, he'll be 'mighty lonely without William,' once the deal's been done."

"And by deal you mean him sellin' me to Lawrence."

"I ... assumed that's what he meant, yes. But ... well, in all my time with those assholes, their ... impulsivity has been clear to me since the start. Without William ... I dunno. I highly doubt Sam would be able to pull something' like this off. 'N fact, there's a good chance he's barely thought it through at all. They relied on luck a lotta the time. Guess that luck's runnin' out."

Morgan exhaled through his nose, not quite a laugh, but close. "Certainly, run out for William."

"Yep. But, as for Sam ... well, even though I'm sure he'll mess this up, he does have a gun. And William's gun. And yours, I guess. Plus, our hands are tied. Not much we can do right now 'cept humor the bastard."

They sat in silence for a while. Then came the inevitable questions.

"So, why'd you want him dead?"

He looked up at Agnes and noticed that her eyes weren't quite so red anymore. This presumably meant she hadn't been crying while he'd been asleep. Either that or she'd cried so much recently that she had no more tears left in her. Morgan hoped it was the first one.

How much did he want to give away? Was there any reason he shouldn't tell her everything? Hell, if Sam really found Lawrence, then this would all be over soon. And if it ended with Lawrence killing him, he wouldn't have to worry about whatever he said to Agnes. If it ended with him killing Lawrence, which would admittedly be his preferred outcome, then he'd have to worry even less.

In the end, he settled somewhere in the middle. He'd tell her the basics if she wanted to know more, and they still hadn't reached wherever they were going, then maybe he'd tell her the rest.

"I'm not quite sure where to start, really," he said, scratching his back for it was all he could reach.

"Beginning's always good."

"Well … we'd been in a sort of gang together, Lawrence and me. Up until a while ago, this was. Neither of us was in this gang willingly, mind you, we'd both … uh … wronged the leader of the gang in some way. And we were serving out our time, so to speak. The alternative was … well, the leader of the gang, the name was Crawley Dalton, horrible old man … he said he'd hurt the ones we cared about. So we worked for him."

"If you don't mind me asking," Agnes said, and paused. They both looked up, it sounded like the horses were slowing. Maybe Morgan wouldn't be telling much of his story after all.

But a few seconds passed, and they were off again, every now and then bouncing when the wheels hit a rock.

"You were saying?" Morgan said.

"Yeah, uh … how did you wrong him? What'd you do?"

"Honestly?" He smiled. "Nothin' much. But he was a hard-old bastard. If you so much as gave that guy a dirty look, you'd be on your knees beggin' god's sweet mercy."

Agnes nodded slowly. He hadn't quite answered her question.

"It's not important. That whole story, quite honestly ... it really only exists to lead into this next story, which will answer your first question."

Agnes bit her lip, thinking back for a second, or perhaps just waiting for him to continue, he'd always preferred reading books to reading people. "Why do you want to kill Lawrence Wildrick?"

"Right. So, we were workin' for this Dalton fella. Wasn't too bad. Most a' the time we were just tax collectors with guns on our belts. Mean stuff, and I ain't proud of it, but the alternative ..." he sighed. "Well, I told ya 'bout the alternative."

He found his eyes drifting down to her bandages. That small circle of blood he'd seen was not quite so small anymore.

"Basically, he liked both of us. A lot a' the time, when Crawley Dalton put strangers to work, they'd be dead by the end of the week. But for whatever reason, he liked us."

"Did you ... sorry to interrupt, but were you close with Lawrence? You talk to him much?"

Morgan laughed. It was a real laugh this time, and it felt rather strange. "Now there's a good question. Yeah, we worked together a lotta the time. I can't say I respected him too much in the beginning, trust me, what he did to piss off Dalton was a hell of a lot worse than what I did, but he grew on me, I suppose. Had my back a couple times. And that sorta leads me to the next part of the story. The only part that really matters."

"Good," Agnes said. "Was gettin' bored for a while there."

He stared at her for a second, and she laughed. "I'm kiddin', Morgan. Keep goin'."

"Oh," he smiled. "Well, as I was sayin', Crawley liked the both of us. But I guess he thought there was only one way he'd know if we could really be trusted. So, he sent us both a message. At the time, neither of us knew that the other had got the same note. Mine said, 'Wild Rick. Can he be trusted?' This was back when he used that awful nickname, mind. From what I heard a little while after, he said the same thing, just with my name 'stead a' his."

"Huh," Agnes said. "So what d'you say?"

"I said yes," Morgan said, and he looked away at what would've been the stars but was instead a dark sheet. "Didn't even hesitate. Cause he'd grown on me, like I said. And ... well, t'tell you the truth I was far more naïve back then than I am today. I didn't think anythin' would come of it.'

Agnes nodded.

"'Course, Lawrence ... he said no," he said. "He had two sons, and I guess ... I guess he'd heard more about Dalton's ruthlessness than I had. So, he said no, I couldn't be trusted. Musta thought that would cement him as a trusted member of Crawley's gang, right? As if it would ever be that simple."

He paused, adjusting his arm a little. It still hurt, but every few minutes Agnes winced, so he counted himself lucky that his own bullet hadn't stuck around.

"So, it wasn't that simple?" Agnes prompted.

Morgan sighed. "No. Actually, it kinda was. It kinda was that damn simple. But there was one more thing. One more test a' trust. Crawley sent Lawrence another note. And I saw him before then, Lawrence, I mean, and we were all smiles, enjoyin' each other's company and whatnot. We had a good laugh that day, from what I remember. I think in some other life ... I think he'd a' made a good partner."

Again, he paused. He was nearing the worst part. The hardest part to speak of, or even to think of. And the closer it came, the more sure he was that he physically couldn't tell Agnes everything, after all. It wasn't up to him. It was up to the darkest corners of his mind, of a gunslinger, and all at once it was screaming 'no.'

"What was on the other note?" Agnes asked.

He sighed.

"Well, I'm not quite sure what the exact words were, but the gist of it was 'cut off Morgan's hand and send it to me."

Agnes's eyes widened before falling into his arms. His hands, or what should have been his hands, were out of view, tied behind his back. The arm she'd patched up when they got in the wagon had been his right one, and that arm still had a hand, so she hadn't noticed any glaring abnormalities.

"Did he?" she began.

"I'd like to think he hesitated. But there's a couple folk back home that ... they say otherwise. They say that the night he got the note, that's when he snuck into my house, tied me down, and chopped off my hand with a rusty axe. So, it was simple. Simple enough."

"My sweet Christ," Agnes whispered.

"I woke up screamin'. But he had a buddy with him, and he covered my face with a pillow so I couldn't see who was there. But I knew. Even in all that shock, all that agony. Could've really been anyone, but I knew it was him. I don't remember this next part, but apparently, I was screamin' his name. Over and over and over. I hope that haunts him. Hope that keeps him up at night. But somehow I doubt it."

Again, silence claimed the wagon. Finally, Agnes said, "And then he sent your hand to Crawley?"

"Mm. Had one of his men come pick it up, the same man who'd delivered me my note back at the start. I liked that fella, too. Name was Henry. Thought he liked me too. But I guess he wasn't in the business a' likin' people. Anyway, from what I heard a while back, Crawley threw the ... my hand in the ocean. I've been usin' this wooden thing since then. Used to know a good carpenter, tracked him down. A fake hand's mighty pricey, but with these gloves, you can barely tell the difference."

Agnes nodded slowly. "So ... was that the last test? To cut off your hand and send it to Dalton? Or was there somethin' more?"

Morgan closed his eyes. The final part of that unspeakable memory, which was in many ways the first part, was the one he'd been blocking out for some time now. But since he realized how close he was getting to the man who'd caused it all, since he realized this might all be over soon, that memory had been clawing its way back in ...

He remembered his wife. The kind, generous, good woman that he'd called his wife. And he remembered the knife, as it ...

He opened his eyes. Far back in the dark places of his mind, he remembered what Lawrence took from him, and he looked at Agnes, and said, "I just want him dead. It's really not all that complicated. He doesn't deserve to walk this Earth, doesn't deserve to feel the sand beneath his feet, or the dirt, or the grass, doesn't deserve to hear the birds, not while my wife ..."

Agnes put a hand on his shoulder, and at that moment he noticed the tear running down his face. She reached forward and wiped it from his cheek. Morgan wondered what would have happened if her hands had been tied behind her back like Morgan's, rather than at her front. He wondered if they'd both be dead by now.

"Okay, Morgan," she said. "I understand."

He nodded, pulling himself together with every moment that passed, and then came the second round of inevitable questions.

"How long had you been with them?" Morgan asked. "Sam and William, I mean."

She gazed down at her feet for a moment. "Three months? I ain't too sure, to be honest."

"Has ... has it been as bad as it is in my head?"

"Well," she said with a small smile. "I'm no mind reader, Morgan. But it's probably pretty close, yeah."

"I'm sorry they put you through that."

She shrugged, shaking her head a little.

"What's done is done, right? I know women who've had it a whole lot worse."

Morgan sighed. "I dread to think."

Then, after a pause, "You want me to kill him?"

Agnes smiled again. "Let's just see how things go, alright?"

"Alright," he said and tried to smile back.

They talked for a little while longer about unimportant things. He asked once more about her time with Sam and William, and she told him that, if there were a chance they'd both be dead in a matter of hours, she didn't want their last conversation to be one of such despair.

Before long, the horses had stopped. They heard Sam hop off the animal, heard him shuffle back to the wagon. He tore the sheet from the cage.

They were outside a house of some kind. It looked fairly run down, as did the small town not too far down the road.

"Shouldn't have to remind y'all not t'try anythin' funny," Sam said, and they obliged, for now.

He waltzed up to the house and wrapped twice on the door. Then, his patience clearly wearing thin—he was pacing back and forth, kicking up dirt with every step—he knocked a third time. To Morgan's surprise, the door opened. It must've been four a.m., possibly even later.

They heard some mumbled chatter, trying to peer through the cage's bars to see who Sam was talking to. Minutes passed, and then the man appeared. He was far scruffier than Sam, but before Morgan said, "Wonder when he last had a bath?" he realized he couldn't quite remember when he'd last had a bath.

The man inspected the pair when he got to the wagon, coughing and spluttering every few seconds. At one point his saliva reached Morgan's clothes.

Then all of a sudden, he was talking again, but this time it was to Morgan.

"Lawrence Wildrick. Wha'd'you want with Lawrence Wildrick?"

Morgan inhaled, unsure how to approach such a delicate situation. "Do you know where he is?"

Sam came into view from behind the scruffy man's shoulder, waving his gun in the air and scowling in Morgan's direction. Morgan sighed.

"I want the man dead."

"Lawrence Wildrick," the man nodded. "You want Lawrence Wildrick dead."

And Morgan nodded.

The man turned back to Sam and said, "Alright. Guess I can tell you where he is. I'm surprised you don't already know, to be quite honest. Ain't too far from here. Just past the town."

"Tell me where is, Branson," Sam snapped. "Where exactly."

Branson ignored him, raising a hand. "The girl. What's her part in all this?"

"Well," Sam said. "I ..."

Branson shook his head and turned to walk back to the house. "Don't worry. I'll take her off your hands. I'll need more rope, though. Those flimsy knots won't do."

Sam sighed. "Fine, fine. Just hurry it along."

When the man was inside, Sam sneered at Morgan. "I am so glad you decided to come into my life, Morgan Meade. I'm about to be a rich, rich man, thanks to you. William'd be proud. Think this is the closest I'll get to avenging that poor son of a bitch."

He chuckled and turned around. It took Morgan a few seconds to realize the man was urinating in the dirt.

Morgan turned to Agnes. She looked across at him, her eyes two globes of despair.

"Agnes," he whispered. "I need you to take my hand."

"Hey, Sam," Morgan called. The man turned, pulling up his jeans.

"The hell would I care 'bout anythin' you had to say t'me? Keep your damn mouth shut."

"You said sellin' me to Lawrence is the closest you'll get to avenging your sick bastard of a partner. But y'know what? I don't think that'd satisfy old William. I mean, I barely knew the guy, but as soon as I pulled the trigger, I could tell what was gonna be the last thing goin' through his mind."

"You keep your damn mouth shut!" Sam yelled, stepping closer to the wagon.

"I could just tell he was thinkin', 'god damn, if the dummy on my right doesn't avenge me good'n proper—"

"You think I give a shit what you're sayin' to me? Think you're gonna get in my head? Ya lost, Morgan! It's over! You—"

"Oh, look at that," Morgan said, peering over Sam's shoulder. "Your friend's back."

Sam turned around, and just as he realized that Morgan had been lying, Morgan sprang forward. Seconds later there was a knife at Sam's throat. The tiny blade had been hidden within the thumb of Morgan's wooden hand. Fake limbs were pricey, he'd been telling the truth about that, but they were a hell of a lot pricier when you wanted a knife in there.

"You son of a ..." Sam spat, but the blade dug into his skin, and he ended his shout in a whimper.

"Drop the guns," Morgan said. "All three of them. Drop them where I can see them."

He could feel the man trembling in his arms. "Branson's gonna kill you, y'know. No way outta this for you."

But he dropped the guns. All three of them. Morgan could see each of them lying in the dirt.

"Wish I was the one holdin' the knife," Agnes muttered.

"Now unlock the cage," Morgan said. "Unlock it. I know you have the key."

Sam sighed. He reached into his pocket, turned a little awkwardly, and then the cage was unlocked.

Just as they had planned while Sam made a river in the sand, Agnes jumped out first, gathering all the guns. Morgan had warned her not use his own gun, the one with the initials scratched on the side, when standing off against Branson, on account of there being one bullet left inside, and he was pleased to see she was heeding his advice. She pointed Sam's own gun right at his shivering face.

"Bitch," he said, and spat at her. She dodged to the left, and it landed not far from his urine.

Morgan jumped out of the wagon, pushing Sam to the ground. Agnes handed him William's gun.

Morgan sighed, with relief this time.

"Well, guess you've played your part now, Sammy."

"No," Sam said, staring up at him, and Morgan realized tears were dripping from his chin. His eyes were red already.

"Please, Morgan."

"Sam, if I don't kill you, you'll be a threat to me for the rest of my life. You may beg me for your life now, like the pathetic little man you are, but one day you'll get over this feeling, and a new feeling will take hold, hatred. Hatred, Sammy. And you'll hunt me down."

Morgan glanced up. Branson was still in the house. Good. He was quite enjoying being able to savor this.

"No," Sam cried. "I won't. Why would I? If you spared me, if you let me live, I'd be grateful forever. I wouldn't hate you. I'd ... I'd love you! You'd be my savior! I'd owe everything to you!"

"It's just not true, Sammy."

His pleading continued, and Morgan gave Agnes one last glance. She nodded.

The gunshot was loud, but it still took another minute for Branson to emerge from the house. He was carrying heaps of rope, just as he'd promised, and when he eyed Sam's body lying bloody in the dirt, he dropped that rope immediately.

"What the ..." he began, but there were two guns pointed at his chest, and so his shoulders slumped.

"Where is Lawrence Wildrick?" Morgan said.

Branson, now trembling much like Sam had been, turned and pointed to a shack not far beyond the town.

"That's where he stays, most of the time," Branson said. "I'm ... I'm a well-regarded man in this town, you know. If something happened to me ..."

"Are you telling the truth? Lawrence Wildrick, he really lives in that shack?" Before the man could answer, he continued. "Branson, if we get to that shack and Lawrence isn't there ... you know I'm gonna kill you, right?"

Alarm lit up Branson's face. "But ... but what if we get there and he's not in? What if ..."

Morgan smiled. "I guess it's just all down to luck, Branson."

"But I ..."

"What d'you say, Agnes? Branson look like a lucky fella to you?"

Agnes shrugged. "Not from where I'm standin'."

"Well," Morgan said. "We'll find out soon enough, I suppose."

They passed the town. It took them twenty minutes. Now and then they saw people milling around, but it was late. The sober were asleep.

When they drew near to the shack, Morgan patted Branson on the shoulder. The man was glancing around, presumably for help of some kind.

"Bet you're considerin' shouting for help, huh Branson?" Morgan said. "I mean, there's some people right back there. They'd probably hear you, even from way up here. And, you bein' a well-regarded man and all, I'm sure they'd come rushing up to help. That sound about right to you?"

Branson nodded timidly.

"'Course, there'd be a bullet in your head long before help arrived. But you knew that, didn't ya?"

Again, Branson nodded.

Agnes stopped. Morgan looked ahead to see what she was gawping at.

It was a sign. Hanging right beside the shack's door. On it were four letters: JAIL.

"Lawrence! Lawrence!" Branson started to scream.

"What the hell?" Morgan mumbled, grabbing the man and putting the gun to his head.

And then he appeared. Lawrence Wildrick. His big black hat covered his forehead, but his eyes were wide and unmistakable. He was holding a gun, not unlike Morgan's own, and beside him was another man, dressed in much the same clothing but for one notable difference. On Lawrence's coat, its face inscribed with one word was a six-pointed star.

"Gotta be fuckin' kidding me," Morgan sighed.

Agnes turned to him and whispered, "He's the sheriff?"

"Well I'll be dashed," Lawrence said. "Thought my eyes were playin' tricks. Morgan Meade. It's been a long, long time."

"Beef him, Sheriff!" Branson shouted in a whisper as if trying to deceive the man with a gun to his head.

Lawrence didn't meet the man's eye. Instead, he stayed fixed on Morgan's, waiting for the man to speak. Finally, he did.

"Sheriff," Morgan said. "Huh."

"Got something to say 'fore we finish this, Morgan?"

"It's just ... well, I knew fine well you traded my hand to Crawley Dalton. Didn't think you'd have sold your soul."

Lawrence laughed. He gave the man on his right a quick glance, and the man—barely a man at all—stiffened his posture a little.

"I'll admit the man helped me get where I am today," Lawrence said. "No doubt about that. But I work hard, Morgan. And I plan to keep workin' hard. You've met my family. Patricia, Dal, Jeff. All I do, I do for them. And that includes what I've done, Morgan."

"Don't know what you're referring to," Morgan says. "Care to be more specific?"

"It was you or me, Morgan. Actually, no, it was your family or my family. My wife, some way pregnant. My son, just learnin' to shoot ... and what were you protectin'? Y'know, I can't even remember her name. But, hell, I'm sure half the men in the state knew her name back then."

What happened next happened quickly. Later, Morgan would assume that Agnes's bullet had been meant for Lawrence. The fact of the matter was, though, that it hit the man to his right. Went right through his neck. A fine shot, a tremendous shot, if Agnes had as little shooting experience as Morgan assumed. It didn't matter who her target had been, in that moment, it was very clear that she'd saved his life.

The next bullet didn't come from Agnes. Nor did it come from Morgan or Lawrence. As the unnamed Sheriff's Deputy collapsed in the dirt with his fingers at his throat, a second gun fired from inside the shack, there had been, of course, a third man in Lawrence's party, one that had stayed inside while the small talk ensued. And it was this man's well-placed bullet that found itself tearing right through Agnes's shoulder.

She dropped to the ground with a shriek, clutching her shoulder with one hand and breaking her fall with the other.

"Stop!" Lawrence yelled over his shoulder. "Hang fire, Dallas!"

He walked toward Morgan, whose gun was still at Branson's head. Morgan backed away, taking the man with him, and Lawrence bent down to pick up Agnes's gun. He threw it to the bushes.

"Morgan, put your gun down. I know you'd rather go out guns blazin' than let me take ya alive, but this woman'll die if you don't give this up right about now."

Morgan glanced down at Agnes. She was in pain, that much was certain, but her eyes were still focused on the task at hand. She stared up at him.

"You're here for one thing, Morgan. Dude's an ass. Take the bastard out."

"Morgan, I don't care if you kill this man," Lawrence said, nodding at Branson. "Tell ya the truth, I ain't even sure if I've seen him before. Couldn't give a donkey's ass whether you shoot him."

Branson whimpered softly.

"If you try to shoot me, I will fire until you are dead. Some of those bullets may pass through Branson. I was never as fine a slinger as you ... well, before the ... the hand."

"You heard her, Lawrence. I'm here for one thing."

Lawrence sighed. "You'll be dead long before you can take your first shot, Morgan. You know that. But so will Agnes, thanks to my in the window back there. Just put the gun down."

"Everything you took from me ..."

Morgan was staring into the eyes of his enemy, but all he could see was his wife.

"Morgan ..."

Before he could continue, Morgan dropped his gun. He pushed Branson to the ground.

Lawrence gave it a second. Then he approached Morgan like one would approach a rattlesnake, if one was ever so inclined.

With the butt of his gun, he struck the man on the head, and for the second time that day, Morgan saw black.

"You son of a bitch," he says.

Lawrence Wildrick sighs back. "Christ, Morgan. I mean, Christ! It was only a hand! And hell, from what I can see you've been doin' just fine without it. Followed me for god knows how long, nearly put a bullet in my head."

"You think it's my hand? You think I went to all this damn trouble for a hand?"

Lawrence leans down. "Well, I sure as shit didn't take anythin' else from you. I'd have remembered if I did."

Morgan stays silent for a few moments, but he has to ask, "Agnes. You kill her?"

Lawrence chuckles softly. "No, I did not kill her. We're keeping her for a little while, though."

"Until you've killed me?"

"Until she's better."

Morgan stares off into the night. Lawrence follows his gaze.

"You're a nice fellow, Morgan. I mean that. And I really ... I really don't wanna kill you here. What I want is to let you go about your business. But I just get this feelin' that ... if I did that, Morgan, then I would wind up dead as your left hand, eventually. Am I right in that feelin', Morgan?"

"Yes."

Lawrence sighs. He looks at his gun. "Why?"

"You wanna know why? You wanna know why, Lawrence?"

"Yes. I really do. Tell me why I have to kill you here, Morgan. It might make me feel a little better about doin' it."

"I never gave two shits about my left hand. Y'hear me? 'Side from the shock of it, I never did care."

"So why?" Lawrence nearly screams.

"My wife. My wife, Lawrence."

"What, you think I killed her or somethin'? That it? Why you bringin' her up?"

"No. No, I don't think you killed her. She ... she was dead a year before I met you. Killed by ... killed by a man with no name, and for all I know, a man with no face."

"You didn't think to mention that back then? Man, I'd have cut off your hand a hell of a lot sooner if I'd known you didn't even have a wife back home. So ... I don't get it, Morgan! If she was dead before I even knew you, then what in the hell does she have to do with this?"

"You cut off my hand." Lawrence's eyes are wide. They look fit to explode. "Let me finish. You know what was on that hand, Lawrence? You know what was on one of the fingers of that hand? Guess. Take a wild guess."

Lawrence takes a second, but soon he understands.

"Alright, Morgan. I see what you're gettin' at."

"My wedding ring. My wife's wedding ring. The only god damn piece a' her that I had left and you took it from me, Lawrence. You took it from me without a second thought."

Lawrence nods slowly.

"That's why you've gotta kill me here. That's why there's no other way."

Lawrence pauses. He looks away, stares off at the sunset for a while. He sighs, looking down at his gun again.

"You lied before," Morgan says.

Lawrence tilts his head.

"You remember my wife's name. You said you didn't, but you do."

Lawrence nods slowly.

"Y'know ..." he starts, but sighs again and looks away. "Y'know I've never ... I mean I've ... killed. Not for a while, though. And I've never ... looked into a man's eyes, before ..."

"I know," Morgan says. He thinks of his wife.

Lawrence stares at the man.

"Alright, Morgan."

There is a brief pause. Then he gets up and dusts himself off.

"Then I guess you win."

He rests the gun's barrel against the man's head. Takes a long, deep breath.
When he pulls the trigger, their eyes are locked.

Naomi

Andrea J. Hargrove

My hand sagged under the weight of the proof in my numb hands, and they fell to my knee as I crouched beside the trunk. As soon as I could hear my thoughts over the drumming of my own pulse, I considered putting it back where I'd found it. I'd only looked because I had to know the truth.

Why did I have to know? Whoever the culprit, the answer to the puzzle could only bring me pain.

I couldn't act on that initial impulse, though. Even if I was the sort of man to conceal a crime, the only movement I could manage was to sink the rest of the way onto the rough wooden planks nailed together to comprise the tent floor. At some point, a sharp breeze chilled my face and brought my head up to stare at the silhouette of the person standing in the doorway, holding back the canvas flap.

"I know how Naomi died," I said, the words pushing through the thick wad of disbelief stuck in my throat.

The silhouette slipped inside and let darkness shroud the tent once more.

I could've spoken about why it happened or how it happened. Instead, I looked down at the thing in my hands, mind working back to where this all began. *Did I miss any signs? Could I have prevented this tragedy?*

The images played themselves out before my eyes like I was still standing there. That happened to me sometimes–had done ever since the war. Sometimes if I sat still too long, the whole aftermath of Chancellorsville would flicker through my mind. Every bullet I'd dug out of the men, every limb I sawed off, every twisted face, and every cry for mercy and choked-off prayer.

This time I didn't go back to a battle. This time I went to Independence, Missouri, April 28, 1866, just as the first orange glow lit the darkness behind us.

Ruth and I kept our light wagon to the outskirts of the slowly-forming party, along with three of our four companions, all former members of the 82nd Illinois Infantry. The fourth, still gathering supplies in town, was a widow of that same regiment. While I wasn't officially attached to any regiment or command, the 82nd Illinois was the company I'd grown most fond of, and they reciprocated. Though their respect for my medical skills was just about matched by their lack of respect for my 'real world' skills, as they called any sort of hands-on activity.

Johnny and Twiggs, with their handcarts loaded and ready to go, laughed as I carefully double-checked and triple-checked the straps on the mule harness. "Gonna shine it, too, Doc?" Twiggs asked, grinning with a mouth that was missing three teeth in the front.

I had polished it the night before, long after I should've been asleep, long fingers anxiously working the tallow into every inch of the thick brown leather with a stained rag. "Better than your squeaky wheels," I retorted. "You know I like to keep things as tidy as ..."

My voice trailed off as another wagon rolled up. A team of six hearty oxen preceded the sizeable transport that creaked beneath its contents, these shrouded by a thick bonnet top, and another four beasts trailed from behind, hitched to the back. Wagons were common enough, though perhaps not ones that were so heavily laden, but what drew my attention was the woman at the reins, Mrs. William Power, or Naomi, as she insisted we call her now that we were all family in her eyes. Her mouth curved into a rare smile as she appreciated the effect her entrance had on me and the other men who had never seen her in anything but an old work dress.

"That's right, gentlemen," she said, swinging down from the wagon to join us on the ground—a feat easily accomplished now that she wore trousers instead of skirts. "We're really doing this, and the trail will like as not change us all. Least it's only changed my clothes so far." She smoothed her jacket with her calloused hands and lowered her eyes as she awaited judgment.

My thoughts ran more along practical lines than fashionable ones, and I stroked my short beard as I faced her. "I told you Ruth and I had a little space in our wagon for your things. How can you possibly afford ...?" With my free hand, I gestured at the massive purchase before me.

"I told y'all I'd come into a little money. I may've understated it slightly. Rich uncle died, surprised me by disinheriting his good-for-nothing sons and leaving ev'rthing to me instead. I've spoken naught but three words to him in all my life, but I suppose I seemed more tolerable than the alternative."

As she spoke, my wife and Lieutenant Cain also drifted closer–the last two members of our small party within the larger company. "Suits you," the lieutenant said, speaking either of the money or the clothes.

Twiggs and Johnny began to circle the wagon, Twiggs whistling in appreciation and Johnny scratching his head. "The shops are open?" Johnny asked. "Ain't even sunrise yet."

"Some are," Naomi replied with a shrug. "They know there's a wagon train headin' out at daybreak. But this here wagon I've kept hidden from you boys all week while I been stockin' it. I wanted it to be a surprise." She took my wife's hand. "Ruth, I do thank you and Ichabod for your offer of lettin' me use a bit of your wagon, but I ..."

A bugle heralded the dawn, and the camp fell into a brief, respectful hush. Even the animals ceased their shuffling for a few moments, and the few babies quit their fussing.

Then the spell was broken, and everyone surged forward. Those who were driving or leading wagons—twenty-three in all—formed a rough line that was filled in here and there by those walking alongside. An explosion of conversation seized about half the train while the other half, myself included, wondered what we were getting ourselves into.

Those of us who had seen war had some idea of how grueling the march would become and how chaotic it would be at first as everyone learned how to unpack at night, break camp in the morning, and generally learn to navigate the frontier. New recruits always worked through that learning curve, unless they died first. Of course, we'd never seen women or children this young go through the process.

This was more than I'd ever done, too, since there'd always been others to handle the supplies, and a lot of this terrain would be new to me. I didn't relish the thought of Ruth suffering, especially later on when disease started setting in. It inevitably crept into any camp, brought on by filthy living and close quarters. It killed twice as many soldiers as the enemy did, with dysentery and typhoid fever being particularly ruthless.

I braced myself for more of the same. These and other ailments and injuries would no doubt be common for the next few months, but I could accept that. I could even accept the deaths of those I failed to save, or so I thought at the time. Little did I know at the time that one death would be completely unacceptable.

I kept a brisk trade as we traveled. I could even afford to hold consults for free, though I had to charge any time I used my supplies or expended a considerable amount of effort. Ruth assisted me as I worked, being a quick learner who wasn't afraid to get her hands dirty, and I was proud of how efficiently she dressed wounds and set broken bones, even if we differed on the subject of payment for treatment.

"This is your business," she insisted. "Your time and your knowledge are your wares, and you shouldn't be giving them away for free." The two of us squatted near the southern bank of the Kansas River, finally alone to coat our wagon with waterproofing wax after nearly a half hour of reassuring an anxious mother that her daughter had a simple cold and nothing more serious. The woman, one Mrs. Anderson, seemed unprepared for hardship, and my pity for her outweighed my desire to prepare my wagon.

Now it was nearly our turn to cross, and my mind was mostly on the wide, treacherous river, but avoiding the conversation wouldn't reassure my wife at all. "Consider it an investment," I said, if she really needed to speak of my profession in such crass terms, calling it a business. "The people here consider themselves lucky to have a doctor with them, and if I prove generous with them, they may reciprocate if we ever fall on hard times."

"No, the people will take advantage of you."

As we finished our work, I asked, "But you don't mind if I go help Naomi with her wagon?" I shaded my eyes against the sun and observed the surprising lack of activity in that direction.

"War widows are different." She frowned and tilted her head as she looked the same way. "Though I am surprised none of her suitors are assisting her."

"Those three? They're not her suitors."

"Why not? She'd be quite the catch."

"She's said she has no intention of marrying again. I thought you were there when we spoke of it." Ruth's raised eyebrow clearly conveyed her thoughts on the matter, but I smiled and shook my head at her before we made for Naomi's wagon. "Have you finished already?" I asked, noting the shining exterior.

She gestured to Twiggs and Johnny, who sat tossing rocks into the frigid Kansas river. Johnny had especial trouble sitting still. "They got me sorted." The two men puffed out their chests proudly while Cain scowled from his own half-finished wagon.

Out on the river, the oxen faltered, and the ferry bearing some of our companions rocked on the white-tipped waves. A gasp rippled through the waiting crowd, and Naomi clutched my arm. Cain rushed to her side and slid a supportive arm around her back. Johnny and Twiggs leapt to their feet, ready to dive in and save anyone who fell overboard.

The scow passengers huddled in the middle of the flat-bottomed vessel as the ferryman urged his animals in the right direction. The mother and daughter I'd seen earlier, along with the rest of the extended Anderson family, clung together, eyes wide. Even after the ferryman corrected the wobbling and the waiting crowd released a collective sigh, the family refused to calm down until they were rejoined with their wagons on the far side of the river.

Naomi took even longer to release my arm, and she stood there shivering as Cain tried to warm her. I retrieved her heavy winter coat from the wagon and passed it out to Ruth so I could retie the ropes that secured Naomi's belongings together. Ruth helped Naomi into the coat while by the river, I heard Johnny's youthful voice let out a nervous laugh. "I'm glad you were ready to help, Twiggs," he said.

"You mean as opposed to saving my own skin?" The retort held no surprise or resentment. A talented tracker and trapper, Twiggs was known more for his stealth than his bravery. "They owe me some money."

"Them, too? That must make half the wagon train by now. How do you manage?"

"Been catching some rabbits, and I don't always make my customers pay up front."

"Mighty generous of you."

Uncommonly generous, I would've said. I guessed Naomi agreed, from the way she stared at them with pursed lips as I climbed out from her wagon. "Sure is," Twiggs continued. "But once we get further along, I'll get some real hunting in, and you're welcome to come."

"No thank ... no, thank you." Johnny paled at the thought, and Twiggs let a smirk play at one corner of his mouth. He knew as well as anyone that Johnny hadn't been the same since the war and that the sound of gunfire was the quickest way to set him off. Twiggs must've been trying to make his competition look bad in front of Naomi. He needed all the help he could get with his bad teeth and a face pitted with smallpox scars, but I lost interest in their conversation—apart from a vague disgust at his tactics that lingered in the pit of my stomach—and turned my attention to the woman herself.

"They made it safely," I assured her, as no doubt Ruth and Cain had been doing.

"Not everyone does. They fall in. They drown. They get all manner of sickness ..."

"That's what we have Ichabod here for," Ruth interrupted with a confident nod. "He'll be here to set things right."

"Unless something happens to him. I'm sorry," she added quickly. "I don't mean to cast a gloom. It's just ..." she huddled closer to Cain's side. "... death's been following me for a while now. First my Billy, then our boys, then my parents. Even my uncle. I'm sorry," she said again, just as needlessly as the first time. "I know no one here's died yet, and I know we're barely two weeks out, but I just can't shake this curse that's been haunting me. If I lose one more, I ... I don't know what I'll do."

Her eyes welled up with tears, but rather than letting them fall, she wiped them away, clenched her fists, and returned to her wagon to inspect my knots.

That idea's not going away any time soon, I mused to myself. *Those beliefs cling to the mind. Now they're in hers, just like they're in mine, and probably Johnny's, too.* He'd never spoken of his exact thoughts, just about his nightmares, his inability to quiet his mind, and his irritable heart syndrome, for which I occasionally offered him some laudanum. I was glad to see that he'd been ready to spring into action at the river—not that he'd ever had any bad experiences around rivers, to my knowledge.

These considerations continued to circle my mind as the scow finally touched the northern shore, to the applause of those on both sides. The ferryman didn't even glance up to acknowledge it. He was too busy unloading, turning, and cutting back across the cold water. His sturdy face held no concern for those people, or for anything but his job, which he attended dutifully. He could've been Charon ferrying the dead across the river Styx for all I knew, and once that comparison struck me that was all I could see. A rust-colored skiff took the place of the muddy scow, the craft manned by a much older ferryman with a long, dirty beard and a keen gaze.

The illusion didn't even break when Naomi returned from her wagon, fist clenching the money she needed to pay the ferryman. "It's my turn next," she said, and she walked to the riverbank to meet him.

Morbid fears of death continued to plague Naomi even as we traveled through the open spaces free from our pasts. She tried to keep them to herself, but there were times she couldn't help herself, especially as we passed the Coast of Nebraska, which divided the Platte Valley from the open prairie. Marked and unmarked graves marred the rolling brown fields and when we made camp there in what was once known as the 'cholera corridor,' it took every ounce of strength for her to keep her composure.

I found her pacing that night under the wide-open stars when a nightmare drove me from my tent to gasp for some fresh, cool air of my own. Sweat dotted my brow, and my pulse skipped as I panted for breath.

"Ichabod?" a tentative voice called. Naomi circled around the tent into view, and her shoulders slumped with relief. "I'm glad it's you."

My fingers fidgeted at my throat, struggling to undo my jacket button until I realized that I wasn't wearing my jacket–just my long johns and trousers. This wasn't my uniform. This was ... I shook myself fully awake and examined my surroundings. "Has someone been bothering you?" I asked.

Naomi's tent sat inside a protective diamond between those pitched by Lieutenant Gideon Cain, Privates Jonathan Walker and Benedict Twiggs, and myself. She should've been as safe as could be, but her eyes lingered on Cain's tent.

I started in surprise. "Has the Lieutenant conducted himself, er, improperly?"

"Not as such. I've just made it clear to all three of them that their advances are unwelcome, but they're all right persistent—Gideon especially. It was poetry tonight. Bad poetry. And I think he'd had a drink too many when working up the nerve." She glanced up at the points of light illuminating the darkness above us. "If I knew about poetry, I'd write about that. Or this." Her hand spread to encapsulate the plain around us, mostly still in the dead of night, and I would've liked to think she was talking about the fields themselves, or maybe the wagon train, but I rather thought she meant the all-present graves. "What about you?"

I considered the question. "I'd write about anything that would help me forget."

"Is that why you're coming West with us? I know the boys were all looking for work, but you have a good, respectable profession. I know you said there was another doctor in town and you needed to find someplace to move on, but I don't see why you'd have to move this far."

"You might be right." I had to admit I'd kept my ears open ever since I was mustered out, waiting for the right group to latch onto. The problem was, most of the men I knew were going out to work on that new railroad that was supposed to stretch from coast to coast, but their camp had to keep moving and moving along with the rail line, and I didn't want to put Ruth through that.

When Johnny Walker started talking, saying his cousin needed workers in some new foundry in Willamette, that sounded just perfect for me. I could hardly run farther west than that, and the town was stable enough that I could start a family there with no fear. Naomi was the same as me, though she was more honest about it.

"Thank you," I said, and she didn't ask for what.

The companionable moment shattered all but a moment after that when a woman shrieked from across camp. We both bolted in that direction–Naomi in her boots and me in my bare feet, and others emerged from their tents as well to flock in that direction.

We found Mrs. Anderson–the woman who'd been on the tipping scow back on the Kansas River–rocking back and forth clutching a little body to her chest. *Her daughter with the cold?* No, the girl was off to the side, buried in the thin arms of her sobbing father. This one was much smaller–a little boy I hadn't seen before. He hung limp, and though his face was buried in his mother's bosom, I had some idea how it would look.

I tried to urge Naomi away while rooted in place myself, but she stared in horrified fascination.

"He was fine this morning!" Mrs. Anderson wailed. "Doctor, he was fine this morning!"

"None of us are fine," Naomi said, which was possibly the worst statement she could've made, under the circumstances.

The whole camp had gathered by that point, from what I could tell, and they all heard her declaration of hopelessness, took it in, and let it take root in their hearts. How much it would grow, only time would tell, but there was no way to take it back. And I could tell Naomi didn't intend to.

Another night, another scream, but this one came from inside my head. The beardless boy on my table, the one peppered with shrapnel, seemed too young to be an officer, even a second lieutenant, but there we were. The wounded were coming in far too fast to handle, and I thought this one was already dead until he made that unearthly sound and grabbed my wrist ... and shook me awake. No, it wasn't the boy. Someone else was shaking me, and I wasn't in Gettysburg, Pennsylvania. I was in Nebraska, somewhere along the Platte River, but I couldn't fully rouse myself, no matter how hard I tried.

The dream was already fading, far more quickly than they normally did, but I lay there drained of all energy with my pulse pounding in my head. "Doc!" the pulse said. "Doc!" Except it wasn't my pulse, it was Johnny, tugging on my arm and urging me up. "Come quick, it's Naomi!"

I couldn't come quickly, but I did come, still groggy from the battle, or at least the stain of its memory. Ruth already had my medical bag and my coat in her hands and was urging me on from behind, nudging when she had to. "What's going on?" I managed to get out.

"Something's wrong with Naomi. She's not ... I mean, she's ... Well, you just need to come."

With that, he got me the rest of the way to her tent and yanked me inside. A woman with wheat-colored hair sat with blood on her body and a knife on the floor next to a sheet of paper. I knew her. Where did I know her from?

I blinked.

Naomi. Of course, it was Naomi. I gingerly felt for a pulse for the sake of formality. "What do you mean 'something's wrong with her'?" I demanded. "This woman's dead!"

The haze of the morning continued to stretch around me while I remained only partly aware. I noticed on some level that Johnny dashed out of the tent and that Ruth's hands flew to her mouth, and she dropped my bag, precipitating the sound of broken glass. I saw other men come and go from the tent, read the farewell note on the floor, and begin to ask each other questions.

"What do you say, Doctor?"

"Hm?"

When my eyes met the trail guide's, he asked again, gently, "Could you and your wife clean up the body before the burial? We should do this as quickly and respectfully as possible despite the circumstances, so I'll get some men together to do the shoveling if you could take care of this."

"Of course," I murmured.

As soon as he left, I began to examine the body, probing with gentle fingers under my wife's concerned eyes. "Ichabod?"

"One moment, Ruth. I think ... Yes, there it is." My fingertips reached a small welt–the sort of injury I feared I would find. "Find the other three. Get them here. Drag them in if you have to."

She obeyed, gone in a flash and back in, well, many flashes, probably. I wasn't sure. I was too busy checking Naomi's body for other injuries, and I was relieved to find none besides the welt and the knife wound through her heart. The less she suffered, the better.

Eventually, Cain and Twiggs entered the tent, followed by my wife, who dragged Johnny Walker behind her. Johnny moaned quietly as he twisted his hat in his hands, and when Ruth released him, he hunkered down in a corner and started to rock back and forth. Twiggs kept glancing at the tent flap, but he wasn't ready to cross Ruth, who blocked the entrance with her hands on her hips. Cain just stared at Naomi with vacant eyes.

"She was so beautiful," he whispered. "She still is."

"I know you loved her," I said. "I know you all did, which is why I asked you all to come here. There isn't any law in this wagon train, and there may be a real threat to us all, so I thought we should all decide together what to do."

"About what?"

"About Naomi's murder."

Their mouths all dropped open as one. "Murder?" Cain demanded. "What do you mean? They found a note. Look here." He brandished the offending paper, holding it between two fingertips to have as little contact with it as possible. I didn't know why he was holding onto it. I suppose someone had to. I squinted at it from across the tent.

"What does it say?"

He drew back, not wanting to read it at first, but eventually he complied silently as I picked up the note. "'I'm sorry I didn't make it to Oregon,'" he read, "'and I'm sorry for all the trouble I've caused, but I thank you for your kindness. Don't worry about me— I'll be with Billy soon. Naomi Power.'"

"It's just a ruse," I insisted with a shake of my head. "Someone else must have left that letter to make it look like she killed herself, but really, she received a blow to the head around the time of the murder, and I doubt she did that herself. It was murder."

I shifted and mirrored Ruth's pose. "She was melancholic."

"I know, but it doesn't matter." Well, it did matter, but it didn't have any weight on the matter at hand. "She was murdered; I'm sure of it."

"Why?"

"She might've been robbed." The theory fell apart as a quick inspection of the room revealed nothing damaged or rifled through. I couldn't think of any other reason, though. She had no enemies, and several friends ready to protect her.

Or were they friends? Naomi had, without meaning to, hurt three of the people in this room, perhaps more deeply than she knew.

I licked my lips and considered the matter as my breath quickened. *Weren't most murderers close to the victims?* "It was probably a robbery," I insisted, "or more likely one that Johnny interrupted when he … came visiting?" I directed this last question at him, but he didn't respond, so I ignored him. "I suggest we keep this to ourselves and stay on the lookout for a thief in our midst."

"Agreed," Cain said with a nod. "If you're right, we have to find this man and bring him to justice."

"Good." Some sort of watch would definitely be required, though I wasn't yet sure what that would entail. All I knew was that I would be watching my three friends very closely and trying to determine whether one of them could be a murderer.

Much as I hated to neglect Naomi, I didn't pay much heed to the brief service. Cain spoke a few words about her life, which brought sorrow to herself and joy to others, and about how it had ended too soon. Redness rimmed his dark eyes, but his voice was steady and strong as he spoke to the crowd. Not many people gathered around the grave, now marked by a simple cross made from plywood scraps.

When Ruth caught my head swiveling around to watch the ten attendees, she said, "They all think she killed herself, and to them, that's worse than the plague."

"You're right. Hopelessness is a tricky disease to eradicate." That wasn't what I'd been thinking on, though. I had originally started scanning the crowd to watch for their reactions, having failed to find any physical evidence of a crime.

While the others were digging the grave that morning, I'd searched their tents for bloody clothes but came up empty-handed. There were ways to avoid stains since Naomi had been unconscious and there was plenty of time to work. For instance, the murderer could've stood behind her chair and reached around with his sleeves rolled up, then cleaned up his arms afterward.

However he did it, it left no trace, so I was reduced to this course of action, watching and waiting. From what I saw there wasn't a single mourner who failed to show some sort of sadness or regret. Even Waylon, the trail guide who lingered nearby to oversee the proceedings, stood with his hat off and his chin down. He'd seen it all before, and he hadn't known Naomi personally, so there were no great shows of grief from that direction, but he did have an air of respectful solemnity.

Of course, none of this meant anything for sure. Even a killer could show remorse, especially if that killer was a rejected suitor with genuine feelings for the victim. I wasn't getting anywhere on observation alone, even as I listened to the graveside conversations. The only one of relevance was the one Cain was having with Waylon about the best way to distribute Naomi's things.

"Unless she had any kin back east or out west, you four have the best claim," Waylon was saying. "Anything you have no use for, you can distribute to others in the train or just dump here. No use carrying excess baggage. Mrs. Bone," he said to

Ruth, "do you think you'll have any use for Mrs. Powers's clothes?" Ruth grimaced, and Waylon was quick to add, "I'm sure she had some ladies' things in her wagon. Didn't mean to offend."

"No, it wasn't her mode of dress. Only the thought of wearing ... Well, I'm sure I could use a few of her things–hats and boots and such, but the shirts and trousers can go to some of the boys in the other wagons if that's what you meant. They're too small for the men."

Waylon replaced his hat and tipped it to her. "I'm sure they'll be much obliged. I'll let you all get on with that sorting, then we can be on our way."

"Food first," Cain said as Waylon ambled away. Now that I thought about it, Cain and the others were being far too practical about this far too quickly, but they were all being equally practical so I couldn't place suspicion on any one of them. True, they'd all seen plenty of death and were trained to stay practical in the face of it, but this felt different.

Meanwhile, as they began the sorting process, the trail guide stopped to talk to Mr. Anderson, who'd been watching the proceedings from a distance with a dark look about him. Anderson had recently held a burial of his own, which could explain his apparent agitation as he spoke in a low but animated fashion.

Eventually, Waylon urged him away, and I wondered if Anderson's mood might have something to do with Naomi after all. He might be angry that she'd killed herself at the death of the Anderson boy since it might spur Mrs. Anderson on to similar action. Then again, I shouldn't assume anything. I left the other four to go after him. Ruth said something to me, probably asking where I was going, so I replied vaguely, "I'll just be a moment."

I'd darted after Anderson, skirting around a team of horses and barely avoiding getting swatted in the face with a tail. "I'm sorry if this is all upsetting you," I said. "If there's anything I can ..."

"Not unless you can get rid of that man."

"Man? What man?" Usually, I've found that when I offer my condolences and assistance, the grieving party doesn't actually require anything. It's never stopped me from asking before, just in case there is something. In this case, it was a request that I didn't fully understand.

A slight southern twang rolled through his voice. He usually masked it as well as he could, but now emotion was rendering that task impossible. "Your Private Twiggs. You must know what he is."

The man seemed to be waiting for a reply, so I tried to puzzle it out. "He's a war veteran. He used to be a farmhand on a little farm just outside of Belleville, Illinois, but it went under a couple years back. What else do you think he is?"

"He's a scoundrel, sir, and an opportunist, and he intends to make his fortune on this journey at our expense." He examined my face, furrowed in confusion. "Did you not know?" I shook my head, so he asked another question. "Do you know who I am?"

"You're a man who wants to start a new life out west, just like the rest of us."

Some of the tension released from Anderson's shoulders and he lead me to a more secluded area of the train. His eyes darted about, but no one seemed interested in us; they must've figured we were still dealing with funeral business. "You are correct about that, but I should've asked if you knew who I was. Once upon a time, I was a gentleman, and then I was an officer in the Confederate army. I still considered myself a gentleman then, although you may not."

Illumination struck. "You're not the only one, are you? There are more former Confederate soldiers here in the wagon train. Did Twiggs find that out? Was that the source of bad blood between you?"

Anderson snorted. "Not only did he find out, but he decided he could profit by it. We're all paying him through the nose to keep him quiet. If we don't, he plans to tell all the people anywhere we go about the war crimes he saw us commit. It's a lie, of course, but he's the victor, so he'll be believed."

"How did he even know who you were?"

"He and I came face to face at the Battle of Wauhatchie. He'd lost his gun and started to run away, and when I tried to shoot him, my rifle jammed. There was a second, though, where we stared at each other, and I'm sure he could never forget my face, close as I came to killing him. We were standing close, too."

"You would have to have been close," I agreed, "considering you fought at night. It's clear that ..." I trailed off, temporarily lost in thought. There weren't many night battles, and I was just as happy without them. My work was hard enough without the darkness obscuring my patients. And the soldiers had a hard enough time distinguishing friend from foe, especially when uniforms diverged from the standard colors. Anderson was still waiting for me to finish my statement, as he stood there with growing impatience. "It's clear that Private Twiggs is taking advantage of you, and I'll try to talk him out of it."

"Mrs. Power already tried, after she heard us arguing back in Independence. She did not take it well, I tell you." That explained the looks Naomi had been giving Twiggs. Could she have finally decided on some course of action to stop him? Maybe he found out and stopped her first. Oblivious to my chain of reasoning, Anderson pressed on. "I tried again last night to make Twiggs see reason. At this point, I see little hope of achieving that end, but maybe he'll take it better from a friend."

I started to leave, then stopped suddenly. "Last night? When were you together? I didn't realize anyone else was awake."

Too exhausted to wonder at my inquiry, Anderson confirmed, "We spent a long time talking, he and I, and we did see most of the party turn in for the night, including Mrs. Power. We might've been the last ones to see her alive." My startled look prompted him to clarify, "She was just disappearing into her tent when I came over to confront Twiggs.

"And then the two of you left together to talk?"

"Yes, we did talk. At length. We were there arguing most of the night."

"Were you still arguing when you heard the news of Naomi's death?" He nodded, and I felt my spirits crushed beneath the weight of disappointment. I didn't want it to be Twiggs or any of the men, but it had to be one of them, and it was better to know. At least I hoped it was. "Well, I'll see what I can do," I said again before excusing myself.

Could I have been wrong? Maybe it wasn't murder. Maybe Naomi had hit her head a little bit earlier than I thought, staggered into her tent, and then ... No, that didn't make sense, either.

"Hey, Doc!" Waylon called, stopping me before I could return to my party. He held a dirty winter coat matted with straw and ripped in a few places. "Someone found this and thought it might've been Naomi's. You can add it to the pile. A wagon ran over it, but I'm sure once it's cleaned and mended it'll be just fine."

Is this a sign that a scuffle happened outside of Naomi's tent? She fought with someone, that person knocked her out, carried her into her tent, and then stabbed her. "Where was it found?"

"Over by your five tents."

"Right, thank you." I didn't see why she would simply drop her coat outside before killing herself; that meant I was right after all, but now I knew it wasn't Twiggs. My head ached, and my body shook when I held the coat, and I imagined someone tearing it from her body in a prelude to murder.

A hand on my shoulder startled me, and thinking about the murderer as I was, my first response was to swing around and sock the other man in the jaw. Cain stumbled back, clutching the side of his face in disbelief. "Easy, Doc," he said, as Ruth gasped, "Ichabod!"

"No, no, it's alright, ma'am; we're all on edge," Cain assured her as I stammered out an apology. He rubbed his black beard and then smoothed it back into place. "We saw you standing here holding that and your lovely wife, and I thought you could use some company."

"That's kind of you, but would you mind if I spoke to Ruth in private?"

"Not at all."

When he was gone, I told her, "I didn't know it was him. I thought it was the murderer." I hadn't shared my suspicions with her that he might be the murderer, mainly because I didn't have any proof–only a vague suspicion about motive–and there were other reasons to kill someone. Sometimes, a man could kill without even meaning to.

"Like Lieutenant Cain said, we're all a mite jumpy right now."

"You don't understand. I thought I saw it happening. But I couldn't have seen it, because I slept the whole night. Better than usual, I thought."

She hugged me close and nestled her head into my chest, crushing the brim of her bonnet and some of her auburn curls. "You just imagined it. You know how you get sometimes."

Unfortunately, I did. "You don't think I could've ... could've actually seen something, do you, and then just forgot? I've seen it happen to a lot of boys in the war ... something bad happened, and they put it right out of their heads. They'd get confused." It wasn't just when they saw something bad, either; it was sometimes when they did something bad. I'd also seen some of them get mixed up in all sorts of ways. Sometimes they would mistake one person for another. Sometimes they got violent.

"Not when you were laying next to me all night. I would've known if you'd gotten up."

I sighed. "You don't always know. You know I get nightmares and wake up a lot, but not always."

"You don't seem confused to me," Ruth decided, releasing me, "just upset. And I think the sooner we leave this place, the better."

"You're right." I held out Naomi's coat, and at first, she recoiled, but then she took it gingerly. "Here, why don't you take this. It was Naomi's ... at least I think it was. I thought it was heavier than this."

My wife shook out some of the straw, letting it drift to join the rest that coated the ground. "I'm sure it'll keep me warm enough. Come along, Ichabod. We shouldn't linger here."

Courthouse and Jail Rocks filled me with a vague sense of unease when we saw them in the distance, two imposing formations that themselves reminded one of the staggering power of the Almighty, while their names evoked the justice of man. Someone ought to be punished for Naomi's death, but it seemed less and less likely that justice would become a reality.

"Those look like a courthouse or a jail to you?" Twiggs called up as we drew nearer the sandy brown landmarks, traveling through the old, well-worn ruts of the Platte River Road. It was Johnny's turn driving Naomi's old wagon, which the two men now shared, so Twiggs was free to roam. "One on the right looks like a man's shoe—pointed to the left, you know."

"I suppose it does."

"What about the rock on the left? What does it look like to you?"

Searching for shapes in rocks was akin to looking for them in clouds—a game I'd often played as a child. It lessened my awe of the monuments before me, but it also cut through my gloom, which may have been the point, so I played along now. "A Mayan pyramid, maybe? Because of the way it's tiered."

He nodded, though, in retrospect, he may not have known what a Mayan pyramid was, and spat to the side to clear the dust from his mouth. "If you say so."

We traveled in companionable silence for a while after that. "I gave their money back," he finally said, avoiding eye contact. "Anderson and the others who paid me already, and I told them all they didn't owe me nothin' anymore."

I felt I'd won that argument too easily and that there might be more trouble from him in the future, but I still offered my approval of his present actions. "It'll make your way easier in our new home if you start out with a good reputation, not to mention easier on the trail."

"You and your reputation," he chuckled. "I ain't gonna deny it's working for you, but let's just hope my newfound charity works out for me and makes them grateful."

He might've been taking the wrong lesson away from this, but at least he'd done the right thing. It helped tremendously that I'd confronted him when he was in the right frame of mind—right after he'd inherited a fifth of Naomi's goods and he could afford to be generous. She hadn't had much cash on hand, only a couple hundred dollars tucked away in an old sock, but the rest of his share he could use, trade, or sell. Naomi probably shouldn't have spent so much of her own inheritance in Independence, since we'd be needing supplies later on, not to mention the tolls for different roads and bridges along the way.

I sighed and slackened my grip on the reins. "You're thinkin' about Naomi again," Twiggs asked, "ain't you?" He spat again, which gave him something to do besides look at me. "Who do you think done it? We've all had our theories, with this person or that person lookin' the wrong way, but you never said." He eyed me shrewdly. "You think one of us done it?"

Avoiding the question, I shifted my numb bottom on the hard wagon seat, my boots scuffing the jockey box as I moved. "I know you didn't do it. You were attempting to blackmail Mr. Anderson at the time of the murder."

"Captain Anderson," Twiggs reminded me. "One of those who fought against us."

"He's not fighting anyone anymore. He's running."

Twiggs shrugged. "So, you don't think I done it. I don't think you done it, neither. No reason to make it look like a suicide then say it ain't."

I made a noise of agreement. I certainly did not recall killing her, but what if I'd gone out of my mind? It wouldn't have been the only time I'd forgotten where I was, though surely if I were going mad, I wouldn't think I was.

No, that wasn't true, either. Some men had their lucid stretches, knew that something was wrong with them, and lay there crying for as long as they could before they were sent back to the lines.

"You must think Naomi rejected one of 'em one too many times, and I agree. Cain could'a easily done it in a fit of passion, an' Johnny could'a done it in a … well … in just a fit. Still," he concluded, "it may be high time you let the matter drop."

"What did you say?"

He raised his hands in surrender. "Hear me out, Doc. I thought the world of that woman, but I think the same of every man I served with. And every man who's kept me alive."

Benedict Twiggs had never made his sentimentalities particularly obvious, but it went without saying for most soldiers. I didn't know everything he'd gone through with Cain or Johnny, though I did know how I'd nursed him through his smallpox–mixing warm milk into his food and feeding him the pap for three straight weeks until the disease ran its course and his scabs fell away. Clearly, he remembered it too, and I had to admit that might have had something to do with his willingness to listen to me in the Anderson matter, despite my suspicions.

"I wouldn't want to see one of them hang," Twiggs concluded. "Not for somethin' he probably didn't even mean. Don't you feel the same?"

"To some extent, but even if the man doesn't hang, I still feel we have an obligation to Naomi to find her killer and to banish the cloud over her name."

"If anyone has an obligation, it's those two other men you suspect of killing her and me. I know you meant to keep an eye on her, but you didn't care for her, not like we did. And I'm telling you, you should let matters lie. All three of us agree, there's no way of finding the truth, not for sure, and you'll only ..." He tensed and swiveled when some movement behind him caught his attention. When he saw it was Ruth, he relaxed again. "You'll only drive yourself to distraction."

"Trying to convince him to leave off thinking about the murder?" Ruth asked him. At his confirmation, she threw up her hands. "Good luck to you. I agree, for what that's worth. It's just as well to let the matter rest if we have no way of learning the truth. We should still keep watch for miscreants, but I don't see what else we can do. She wouldn't want us to suffer, anyhow. Not about this. She's happier where she is now, and I think she'd like us to remember that."

It was easier said than done, but I had to acknowledge the truth of their words. "You're probably right, Ruth. You often are. Now, didn't you say you'd be back walking with the Andersons today?"

"Mm-hm, but Anabelle said her daughter's been running a fever and so has the little Downer girl, so she wanted me to ask you if you'd noticed anything going around."

I shook my head. "Nothing in particular, just the usual run of colds, but I can take a look at her when we make camp tonight."

"Thank you. I'll let her know."

"You don't mind my seeing patients for free, now?" A bemused smile crept across my lips.

"Well, you just acknowledged that I'm often right. It's only fair I say you're sometimes right, yourself." She left with a playful swish of her broadcloth skirts. Maybe she had fewer money concerns, too, just like Twiggs. Or maybe I was being unfair to them both.

I wiped my puffed, sleepless eyes and nodded drowsily. "I can let it go," I said again, hoping that speech would give it reality, or at least give me resolution. Then I rode silently to the Courthouse and the Jail.

We'd almost arrived. After prairies, deserts, mountains, and all manner of weather difficulties, reaching the base of Laurel Hill one clear October morning gave me a kind of high I didn't think was going to go away on its own. It would take a truly momentous tragedy to shake me from my bliss.

Some of the others were still coming since we couldn't all make it down at the same time, so I stopped to inhale the scent of pine, to appreciate the song of the birds overhead, and to occasionally glance up and wish my fellow migrants well. Some of the men let their wagons down one chute after another. On the route that we were taking, we could only get them down these vertical descents by securing the wagons with ropes and chains, wrapping the other end around trees and stumps, and lowering their cargo carefully.

My part was done. My arms, back, and legs all wobbled and ached, but it didn't matter while I sat there in a nice mossy patch, warm in the sunlight and free of all responsibility, boots laying beside me.

"Waylon says that's it. That's the hardest part of the trail," Johnny told me hopefully as he paced nearby.

"Good." I wanted to tell him to sit down, but I yawned and lay back the rest of the way to the ground as my triumph faded into a gentle euphoria far more quickly than I'd anticipated.

My eyelids drooped shut, and my head fell to the side. I don't know how long I dozed, but it was peaceful and pleasant and far too short. I awoke when an eleven-year-old boy stood over me, shaking me with tears in his eyes.

"Pa's been hurt," the boy blurted before I even had the chance to lift my head all the way. This child was the son of James Downer, a retired Confederate sergeant, and his hands and shirtsleeves were stained red with what I had to assume was his father's blood.

"What happened?" I asked as I sat up, moss sticking to my unkempt hair.

"He cut his leg on the way down Laurel Hill earlier today. Ma dressed his wounds, but they won't stop bleeding."

"Another Johnny Reb," Twiggs muttered under his breath.

I ignored him and tugged on my boots. "Where's Ruth?" I asked. "She has my bag."

Twiggs shrugged, pleased enough with the world after making it down Laurel Hill but in no ways more helpful as a result. I sought elsewhere for information, and Cain offered, "Tending a sprained wrist, last I knew. In that direction." He pointed toward a huddle of women, which no doubt had Ruth at the center.

Before I could say anything, the Downer boy dashed off to retrieve the bag. "I'll meet you at your wagon!" I called.

Tying my shoes took longer than expected, and I rose with a groan. At last, I got halfway up and had to catch my breath as I stood doubled-over on the side of the path. It seemed I was the only one who heard Twiggs speak. Johnny and Cain still remained ignorant concerning the pasts of our traveling companions, which was definitely for the best.

When I finally staggered over to an extremely mortified Sergeant Downer, I found him sitting by his wagon with his leg propped up on a log, applying pressure to a bleeding cut. His wife sat a little ways off, clutching her stomach and fanning herself. "It's not as bad as all that," Downer drawled. "My wife has a tendency to believe the worst, even though we've gotten this far."

"We can't let our guards down, James!" His wife snapped the words out at a shrill pitch. "The worst could strike us at any moment!"

A grunt echoed through my tired body as I knelt beside him. "Since I'm here, I may as well have a look. Ah, here comes your boy. Careful with that!" I told him, though I was still too relaxed to be anxious. I had already lost a few items when Ruth dropped the bag a few months past, but I'd managed to replace most everything between our stops at Fort Laramie and Fort Hall. I always pack carefully, but when dealing with glass bottles on long journeys, one had to expect the occasional mishap.

The boy stopped sprinting and finished the rest of the trip cautiously while I rolled up his father's pant leg and unwrapped the old bandages. "It doesn't look too deep," I said, turning the leg around in my hands to closely examine the long gash, which was still embedded with some dirt and even a few pebbles. "Still best to get that bleeding under control, so I'll just clean it out again and apply some alum."

"We have some bandages in the wagon," Downer said, and his boy scurried to fetch them as soon as he'd set down my bag with exaggerated slowness.

He hoisted himself into the family wagon and began to search for supplies while I worked to cleanse the wound before me. Voices attracted my attention, and I listened to the boy bickering with his sisters. "Help me look for bandages!" the boy insisted.

"That's your job! Ma told me to finish patching this before we get moving again. Did you even finish picking up the money like you were supposed to before you started running around?"

"Pa's hurt!"

"He says he's fine. Look! You're sitting on them, stupid."

The exchange left me curious, and I asked without thinking, "Did you lose some money on the mountain?" Downer's wife squared her shoulders and lifted her chin, and I immediately withdrew the query. "I apologize; it's none of my business."

"It's alright," Downer said to the both of us and then added to his wife, "If it weren't for Doc Bone, we wouldn't have that money back in the first place." He glanced from side to side and lowered his voice. "I wasn't the only one who slipped on the mountain. The missus fell, too, and she accidentally ripped her skirt. She's been keeping most of our spare cash sewn inside it, so we had quite the time gathering it all up before many people saw. I do believe we retrieved it all, thanks to the quick work of my children."

"That's very clever of you. I just keep mine in an old tin."

He beamed at me but admitted, "It's not so clever. A lot of people do it."

Just like that, my cheerfulness vanished. The weight that took its place blackened the day and robbed me of whatever peace I'd managed to find on the Oregon Trail. "Doesn't it ... doesn't it weigh a lot?"

"Not with the little that we carry."

His wife swatted his arm with her fan, and I struggled to keep my composure as I ran through the actions that were so familiar to me. He still noticed, which should not have surprised me, and he asked, "Everything alright, Doc?"

"It's fine," I replied automatically, then clarified, "I just remembered something, or rather, something makes sense now that didn't before, and it made me think of something I'd been trying to forget."

He caught the meaning of my ramblings even if the words themselves weren't making sense. "It strikes me, too, sometimes," he said softly.

It was the coat. That coat of Naomi's that someone took and then left on the ground ripped up. It had really been a robbery after all. Not love. Not insanity. Just greed. It could've been almost anyone in the camp. I could've cried with relief.

Actually, I found that I was crying, so I awkwardly wiped away my tears and left the Downer family as soon as possible. I had to clear my head, had to think. What could I do, even now?

The wagon train had almost reached Oregon City, and once there, most of us would part forever. My friends and I would head up to Portland, to the Willamette Iron Works, but at least we were staying in the valley. Many of the others would scatter across the state.

I needed to find the money before that happened so I could find the culprit, but I didn't have the time or opportunity to do it. Even if I recruited the other four, there would be a lot of places to search. I hadn't realized before just how many nooks and crannies could hide money. Besides that, it would be impossible to prove what money was lawfully theirs and what was stolen. It would be the same if I tried to watch everyone's spending habits when we got to town. That meant I was back where I started.

Except that I wasn't. Now I knew that my friends weren't murderers. I'd owe them an apology if they'd known my thoughts on the matter. Well, they still merited an apology, though I wasn't sure when or how to deliver it.

For the moment, I only staggered back to the mossy patch where Twiggs, Cain, and Johnny were all still waiting, and I collapsed there with mingled relief and frustration. Then I let sleep overtake me once more.

When our wagon train parted, as I knew it would, that feeling of helplessness welled up once more, threatening to drown me in grief at my own inaction. I'd failed Naomi, I'd failed myself, and I failed our friends. I'd let a murderer go free.

I couldn't say why I'd taken this case as a personal responsibility, other than the fact that I was the first who knew she'd been murdered. Other than the fact that my friends had been completely devoid of ideas. Other than the fact that they all accepted too quickly that these things just happened. And other than the fact that I had been the first to suggest inaction, so that we not alert the killer, and that it was hard to get momentum from there.

I should've confided in all of them sooner, and maybe they would've helped me track down the killer from the start. As it was, I couldn't look any of them in the eye from Oregon to Portland.

They tried to coax me back to myself, but it wasn't possible. I would call it moping, but that doesn't seem to be the right word. I'd barely call it living.

We all set up our tents outside of Portland, and since we intended to be there a few days while they searched for houses and I thought about setting up my business, we all gathered wood to give them some nice flat bottoms and to keep them out of the mud.

"Not much worse than a muddy tent," Johnny said with a shudder as he squinted at some approaching rain clouds.

They all nailed faster while Ruth helped me finish ours. She ended up doing most of the work while I stared off into the distance with the hammer lolling from my hand and then half-heartedly helped her haul some of our belongings inside the tent. "You can't keep going like this," she whispered, kissing me gently as the first raindrops began to patter on the canvas above us. "I know you think she needs you, but I need you more."

"You're right again." I returned the kiss. "Tomorrow morning, would you mind running into town with the other three to get some supplies? I'd like to get some sleep."

"That would be a good idea if you were able to sleep."

"I'll take a bit of laudanum before bed. That should help." I'd never used it myself, but I'd given it to enough patients to trust in its effects, despite her wary frown.

"Just be careful."

"Always."

There was no time like the present, so once we'd rolled out our mats, I took a bit of the laudanum–a mixture of opium and alcohol with a slight flavor of cinnamon. It went down easily enough on its own, though I could've put it in a drink. I wasn't thinking about the drug too long, though, before it started to take effect, pulling me deep into a pleasant stupor that was soon replaced by sleep.

My dreams that night, realistic and bizarre, stretched on and on, and I still remembered them all when I finally crawled back to consciousness. It was well into the next morning, and I had no intention of rising any time soon with that thick cloud still over my head.

Instead, I lay there until I was overwhelmed with a sense of déjà vu. I'd felt this way once before, on the morning I'd found out about Naomi's death. With this thought, I rolled onto my belly, buried my face into my pillow and moaned. It hadn't taken long at all for me to work my way around to her death.

Then again, it still bore consideration. *Did I take some laudanum that night and then forgotten about it? That isn't a good sign. Would I have noticed the next time I went for that bottle? No, that bottle broke when Ruth dropped my bag.*

As soon as I thought the words, I saw it again; Naomi's bloody body, Ruth coming in, the bag dropping, glass shattering.

With that sound, something else shattered inside me as well.

The last piece of the puzzle fell into place, and I flew to my wife's trunk to tear through her clothes at a feverish pace that surprised even myself. *She couldn't have done it. Why would she? Naomi needed us, needed friends. Was it for the money?*

Naomi almost certainly had money missing, money that was sewn into a hidden pouch in her coat and then taken on the night of her murder.

Was it out of compassion? Naomi had spoken with myself and with Ruth on many occasions about the horrors she felt pressing down on her. We both knew that the death of the Anderson boy at such a time had been almost impossible for her to bear, but that felt more like a justification than a reason.

Really, neither one was enough of a reason to kill someone. At least it wasn't for me.

I had my knife out and was ripping through the fabric. Piece after piece of clothing, most of it Naomi's, fell victim to the blade as I kept shredding. I only stopped once I reached Naomi's winter coat.

I removed it from the trunk gently, respectfully, and weighed it in my hands. It was heavy.

How brazen did my wife have to be, to put the money back in the place where she stole it from? I'd never seen her wearing that jacket, though. She'd barely wanted to touch it when I'd first handed it to her. *Was it out of guilt?*

After she'd realized where Naomi kept her money, and after she'd gotten to the point where she thought she could justify her crime, she'd committed cold-blooded, premeditated murder. She'd drugged my food or drink to keep me asleep, knocked Naomi on the head, stabbed her in the heart, stolen her money, faked a suicide note, and then came back to our tent to lay down next to me.

Had she managed to sleep at all that night? Or had she waited anxiously for someone to visit Naomi's tent, to try to wake her and then find her corpse inside.

Or was I imagining all of this? A heavy winter coat might just be a heavy coat. There was only one way to know for certain.

The tip of my knife settled against a small bulge on the inside of the coat, and then it sliced through the fabric to unveil a small deerskin pouch. I pulled the pouch free and tossed the knife and coat aside, to land amidst the mess that was strewn about the floor around the trunk and all over our sleeping mats.

Fingers trembling, I untied the knot that held the pouch shut, and then I pulled the lip open and peered inside. There it was. A wad of bills and a collection of coins that I suspected would add up to more than I kept in my old tin, if I stopped to count it.

I did not count it. Instead, I crouched there by the trunk wondering what to do next.

I still didn't have the answer when the tent flap opened, or when the silhouette of a murderess appeared before me.

The Varmint Man

E. W. Farnsworth

The day the varmint man rode into town, clouds threatened monsoon. Dust came an hour after he passed my ranch. It was two miles high and extending in an east-west line to either horizon.

When the dust storm hit, winds blew every which way and sometimes in whirlwinds. Lightning filled the skies. When the rain came, it hit like wet sand leaving tracks of dust tears on barn sides, houses and wagons.

The haboob shut down all vision for three hours. When it cleared, it was night with a billion stars. The desert smelled fresh and pungent. A full moon glowed.

By then I had forgotten about the varmint man. I took stock by torchlight. Two Palo Verde trees and the long, slanting Mesquite had fallen in front of the house.

The roof held. The barn held together too. The farm animals were restless but unharmed.

When the monsoon comes, dogs and cats go berserk. In the aftermath, I often had as many as a dozen strays sneak by to eat from the trays of food and bowls of water I set out for all takers. Men, women, and children sometimes drop by too, but I have loaves of bread, cakes, and pies for them.

This time, the Logan family stopped by as their house had been crushed by a whirlwind. I fed them a hot dinner of bean stew, served picnic style.

In the middle of the meal, the varmint man rode up and stood watching the feast.

"Don't just stand there, Mister. Serve yourself and take a seat. Only the quick are fed."

"Thank you, Ma'am. I don't mind if I do help myself." He used the ladle to fill a bowl with steaming hot bean and bacon stew. He tore off a hunk of bread from a wheaten loaf. As he ate, the Logans watched him warily.

Clem Logan said, "It's not a good season to be traveling. You're lucky to have survived the storm. We weren't so lucky. The winds pulled our house down. We're going to have to start all over again tomorrow."

"Maybe I can help you put things back together," the varmint man said as he spooned the bean stew under his mustache and into his mouth. The Logans looked at each other in disbelief.

"We can't pay for your labor, but thanks for the offer, just the same."

"You don't have to pay me any money. Just remember I helped when you needed it and pass it on when another needs help as you do now."

Clem said, "I won't take your charity."

"It's not charity, exactly. It's what folks do where I come from."

"Where do you come from, Mister? And what's your name?" Logan's wife asked.

"I'm a long way from my home in Minneapolis. My name's Nick Nicholson. Folks call me Nick 'the varmint man.' You can call me that too."

"Well, Nick, your people must have been some of the first settlers in Minnesota."

"That's right. We built a sod house as fast as we could and barely survived that first winter. I decided I'd rather seek warmer surroundings while the others stayed put. So here I am looking to establish myself."

"It's hard living here in the Territory, Mr. Nicholson. It may not be as cold in winter as where you came from, but it's as hot as Hades in the summer sometimes."

"Ma'am, I'll take my chances with the hot weather. What I've been through prepares me more for Hell's fire than for Heavenly light."

I asked, "Why do folks call you 'the varmint man'?"

Nick finished his stew and used a crust of bread to scour his bowl.

"Ma'am, I take care of pests. If you have an infestation, I find a way to clear it out."

Clem said, "You'll have plenty to do here in Arizona, but the pests in these parts are nothing like what you had in the Mid-West. We've got scorpions and tarantula spiders, rattle snakes, Gila monsters, rabid coyotes and all kinds of insects, like golden wasps that swarm."

"I'm a fast learner, Mr. Logan. All I need is a chance."

I said, "Some of the worst pests in the region are humans."

"Give me some examples."

"Well, we have renegade Indians, plain-old outlaws and murderers from both sides of the Mexican border, half breeds like Comancheros and the thuggish enforcers of the railroad combines and other big interests."

"I may not be able to help with those pests."

I turned up my nose and sniffed at him. He was unsettled by my reaction.

"I didn't say I wouldn't help. I only said I may not be able to help. Surely you've got lawmen to tackle the human pests?"

I nodded. "We have a local sheriff and his deputy. Then there's the marshal and his deputies. Finally, we have the US Army's cavalry. But Arizona's a big territory, and our law-and-order community is spread way too thin. By the time the word spreads about a robbery or killing, the criminals are long gone."

"Carrie, why don't you tell him about your husband Sam," Clem said.

I sighed and turned to Nick. "A group of five bad men raided this property and killed my husband while I was buying supplies in downtown Gilbert. When I came home, my husband was spread-eagled on the porch. They had shot him a dozen times and left him for the flies. They stole our small herd. Fortunately, they didn't burn the house and barn or steal the supplies."

Clem said, "We helped with the burial, but there was no way to guess who'd committed the crime. The list of suspects was far too long."

"Were arrows used? Was your husband scalped?"

I said, "No arrows. His hair was still intact. I don't think the killers were Apaches if that's what you're thinking."

Nick nodded. He said, "I'll look into the matter, but I can't make any promises."

I looked him in the eyes. He seemed honest and concerned.

"If you ever find out who killed my Sam, I want to be part of the hanging party."

"I assume you can ride and shoot?"

Clem answered for me. "Nick, don't let this woman fool you. She's a quicker draw and better shot than most men in Gilbert. Before she married Sam Wells, Carrie rode with the Indians. She can read trails like a book. Some say she can read minds."

I laughed and shook my head at his nonsense. I got practical.

"Logans, you can sleep in the bunkhouse tonight. Milly, grab some blankets from the hall closet. Mr. Nicholson, if you don't want to sleep under the stars, you can use the bunkhouse too as long as you give the Logans privacy. You're welcome to stable your horse in my barn."

"Thanks, Mrs. Wells, for dinner. I'll want to repay you by helping you chop up your fallen trees in the morning. As for tonight, my horse and I will sleep under the stars."

"Okay, but watch out for relocating scorpions on the march and rattlers wanting to get warm and dry. As you've probably already learned, Arizona's pests will come to get you."

Nick, the varmint man, led his horse into the dark. Clem and his family went to the bunkhouse with my blankets. After I cleaned up from dinner, I went to bed dreaming of infestations. I had an inkling this man Nick might help me get revenge for Sam. No one else had volunteered to help me with that. I hoped the varmint man would not turn out to be a varmint himself.

The next morning at daybreak, I heard the sound of an ax hitting wood repeatedly. Looking out the front door, I saw Nick chopping up the fallen trees. I quickly got dressed and made coffee.

I took a cup and a crust of bread to Nick for his breakfast. He stopped using his ax to accept the food and thank me. He ate quickly and drank his coffee in slurps. He got right back to work. I liked the way he swung the ax. He was a tall, lanky, strong man, like Sam had been. The more I watched him, the more like Sam he seemed to disport himself.

Clem came to help Nick with the trees while the other Logans rode back to the wreckage that used to be their home.

"Nelly, we'll be there as soon as we finish," Clem called as his wife and children rode off the Wells Farm.

She called back, "Meanwhile, the children and I will sort through what's left of our things."

At noon the fallen trees were stacks of drying firewood. Nick and Sam rode to the Logan ranch. I had a hundred chores to finish, so I bustled. Then I rode to the Logan ranch where Nick was plying his trade.

Nick shot his pistol at something on the ground. Closer up, I saw he had shot the head off a sidewinder.

"Lunch!" Nick said with a smile and a wink at me. I made a fire and cooked the snake meat as a treat we all shared.

The Logan farmhouse had been torn apart, but its foundations and roof beam were still in place. The four walls were largely intact but offset and flat on the ground. The roof was in two flat pieces as if some huge hand had carefully lifted them from the roof-tree and laid them on the ground.

Millie and I helped the two men raise the walls perpendicular to the foundation. I fetched a rope from my place for pulling the Logans' roof back together. By late afternoon, the Logan farmhouse was functional as a dwelling again.

Millie did the miracle of preparing dinner for everyone out of her supplies that had survived the storm.

"It'll be a good thing if we don't have a second storm after the first. I might cry to see the house disjoined again."

By sundown the work and our meal were done. Clem was grateful and wanted to give Nick something for his help. Nick repeated his words of the night before. He said a simple goodbye and headed toward the center of town while the Logans bedded down in their own house, and I rode home to bed down in mine.

Three weeks went by before I saw the varmint man again. I was buying flour and gingham material at Hasting's General Store. Old man Hastings gestured toward the window.

"It looks like trouble is brewing."

Through the window, I saw some rough looking men in the street. They were trying to give Nick a hard time. I walked out on the wooden walk with my goods to see what was happening.

"Varmint man, you're supposed to be a great shot. So why don't you draw?"

The speaker was dark and ugly. His hairy hand was raised a few inches above his gun. I could see the gun was not tethered. I guessed he was used to doing a quick draw.

I scanned the man's four steely-eyed companions. They formed an arc around their leader. They wore one or two guns each, and two of them carried Henry rifles.

"I'm not looking for trouble, Mister, but you'd best not press your luck. If you pick a fight, I'll do what's necessary to defend myself."

The taunter laughed. "Boys, he says he'll do what's necessary. Isn't that a joke? Are you going to exterminate us like a nest of termites?"

One of the men with the rifles said, "Jake, we're five against his one. What's varmint man going to do?"

"What do you say to that, varmint man? What are you going to do?"

Nick nodded at me. "Why don't we let the lady get by with her things and go home. She has no part to play in our business. There's no reason she should witness what's going to happen next. What do you say, Jake?"

"She's not squeamish, varmint man. Why, that woman's already seen what happens to a man who takes Jake and his boys on single-handedly."

The five men laughed viciously. Jake spat on the ground and continued chewing his tobacco.

I set my purchases on the porch and stepped down into the street. I happened to be wearing my six-shooter. I freed the trigger from the trigger guard and worked my right hand so it would be limber in the draw.

"Are you the five who killed my husband?" I asked the man called Jake.

Jake looked around. "I guess we spilled the beans, didn't we, boys?" He turned to me and said, "So what if we did kill yer man?"

"Then today you'll meet your maker for judgment," Nick said.

I don't know who drew first or second. When I saw Jake reach for his gun, my instincts kicked in.

I drew and picked my targets. I was aware that Nick was shooting too, but I kept my focus on the five bad men. Any of them left standing would be too many.

When the shooting stopped, five bad men lay dead on the ground. Nick was checking the bodies for signs of life. I put my gun in its holster and picked up my purchases.

"Have a nice day," Nick said looking up from Jake's lifeless body. The sheriff and his deputy were coming to see what had happened. As usual, they were much too late to be helpful.

"What's going on here?" the sheriff asked, his gun drawn and his chest stuck out.

"Holster your weapon, Sheriff. The shooting's over. These five men tried to kill this woman. They murdered her husband and wanted to finish their dirty work. She took care of business in self-defense. Now she's going home. Do you have any objections?"

As he holstered his weapon, the sheriff said, "I'll need someone to write a statement and sign it."

Nick said, "I'll be happy to do that. I saw the whole thing. Three of those bodies are lying there on account of my having killed them."

I watched as Nick went with the sheriff and his deputy to their office in the jailhouse.

I rode home thinking nothing of the matter except my Sam had been revenged. My gun had put down at least two of those killers after they confessed to their crime. My conscience was clear.

When I reached home, I felt as if a great load had been lifted from my shoulders. I never thought I'd get the chance for revenge. Nick was the key to why it had happened. He had, indeed, helped me identify and clean the world of those five varmints.

The varmint man had lived up to his nickname.

I was so exhausted, I collapsed in my bed without removing my gun belt. I slept deeply for the first time since Sam was murdered.

Before I awoke, in a dream I saw Sam smiling broadly and shaking his head.

"You killed them. I can rest now." Sam told me. "Go on with your life now. I wish I could be there with you as we had planned. Goodbye."

My eyes were full of tears when I looked in the mirror. Night was falling. A coyote howled in the distance. I wondered whether I would ever see Nick again. Was that thought a betrayal of my love for Sam? I did not think so.

Farming takes every hour of the day and most of the night. After Sam died, I worked alone to make it work. I wanted to hire hands, but I had no ready money—not yet.

I heard in town that Nick's services as an exterminator were in demand.

Clem had given Nick a couple acres of his land so he could build a shack. Nick wasted no time doing what he did best.

When I finally had the time to visit, Nick had made that small patch of wasteland into a comfortable though modest homestead. At the back of the property were six hives for the honeybees he had harvested as part of his varmint business.

"I just stopped by to thank you for all you did for me."

"I did nothing out of the ordinary. You took the best shots. I just made sure you weren't outgunned."

"How did you find those evil bastards? How did you know they were the men who killed Sam?"

"I just got lucky. I lucked out again when the sheriff and his deputy believed my story about how those five men lost their lives."

"Wasn't it plain for all to see?"

"I've known the plainest killing to become a hanging matter. As for Jake and his four pals, they all had friends. Let's hope they don't pay us visits. Their kind knows no sense of fair play and no forgiveness."

"Thank you, Nick. That's a perspective I didn't have."

"So, watch your back, Carrie. If you ever need help, just ask. I could come to live in your barn for a while if you're ever in danger. We make a great shooting team."

I tipped back my hat and said, "I'll remember your kind offer, Nick. Are you doing all right with your business?"

He gestured toward his beehives. "I live in the land of milk and honey."

"I see where you get the honey. How do you get the milk?"

"I trade honey for fresh milk. Every time I clear out another swarm, I build a new hive. Things are going swell. How about with you?"

"I get by. I still can't afford to hire hands. But one day I'll do that."

"And in the mean time, you'll work your fingers to the bone."

"Hard work never hurt me—or you. Speaking of work, I've got to get back to the ranch. I don't mean to be forward, but why don't you stop by for a meal now and then? I'd like the company."

"Thanks for the offer. I'll do that, Mrs. Wells."

"It's Carrie, Nick. Just plain Carrie."

"What's certain, Carrie, is you're not plain."

My heart skipped a beat. *Surely I didn't come all the way here to hear Nick's flattery?* Yet my right hand went straight up to my hair, and my eyes found the ground. I don't know whether I was blushing, but I felt hot all over, and a tingle ran down my spine.

"I'll be seeing you, then, Nick."

"Yes, you shall, Carrie. Ride safe."

I started to ride, but I looked back to see his eyes following me.

The Apache wars were an ebb and flow thing. Months would go by with no incidents. Then out of nowhere a renegade band of Apache braves would raid a farm and steal the livestock leaving the ranchers dead and scalped.

Apaches raided Clem Logan's place, killing Millie and the children. They stole his herd of twenty cattle and burned his house to the ground. Nick had been away during the raid, so Clem had to do all the fighting.

I rode over to see what I could do. There I found Nick helping Clem bury his dead. Clem was beside himself in grief. He wanted revenge in a way I understood.

While he plotted revenge, he lived with Nick. I was there on and off for the week it took them to plan. From their conversation, I could tell that neither man knew anything about tracking Apaches.

"If you go after those Apaches, you'll both be killed for certain."

Nick asked me, "Is it true you learned to track like an Indian?"

"It's true. And you've seen me fight."

"So, if we three should go up against these Apache braves, what kind of a chance would we have?"

Clem said, "I'll die fighting them."

"Spoken like a fool looking to die, Clem," Nick said.

I said, "We'll need to powwow with an Apache squaw I know. Her name is Dahteste. I can arrange the meeting."

"If she's Apache, won't she tell the others?" Clem asked.

"She's not what you think. Dahteste scouts for the US cavalry. She taught me everything I know about tracking. And she has a powerful friend."

Nick was sharpening his Bowie knife on a strop. "Set up the meeting. We'll all go."

The next morning, I rode toward Superstition Mountain. I left signs where Dahteste would find them. It might take a week or two, but she would answer me.

At midnight two weeks later, Dahteste came to my ranch. When I awoke, she was standing quiet as a stone beside my bed. I smelled her presence.

She whispered, "You made the sign. I'm here. What do you need from me?"

"I need to bring two men to meet you. We three need advice about how to handle a band of marauding Apaches."

"What are these braves to you?"

"They killed my friend's family and stole his livestock."

"You know a war is going on."

"Yes. I also know about losing loved ones."

Dahteste nodded and said, "Meet me two nights from tonight at the entry to Superstition Mountain. You know the place. Come with your two male friends and no others."

"We'll see you there, then."

Dahteste vanished.

At daybreak I rode to tell Nick and Clem about the meeting. Nick was satisfied. Clem was not.

"What if she arranges an ambush?" Clem asked.

"She would signal me if any of her fellow Apaches planned that."

"I'm not sure one Apache is any better than another," Clem said.

Nick saw the look in Clem's eyes when he said this.

"Clem, if you're going on a killing spree to kill just any Apaches, deal me out."

I saw the drift of Nick's thought. "Deal me out as well if that's all you intend to do. Do we want justice against the braves who killed your wife and children, or wholesale murder of any Indians we happen to find in our way?"

Clem looked down, ashamed. "I want justice, not murder. I hope I can restrain my desire for vengeance while we have this meeting with your Apache friend."

I told him, "If you can't or won't restrain yourself, I'll kill you myself. Is that understood?"

Clem nodded, but he still seemed not to be convinced.

I said, "I felt as if I could kill every outlaw in the Territory for murdering Sam. I got lucky. Nick found the five men who killed him. We both took care of them in broad daylight."

Clem said, "That's the way I want it to be for the Apaches who murdered my family."

"Good. Trust me. Trust my Apache friend. We'll get to the braves who killed your family. If we go off half-cocked, we'll do no more than stir the flames of this perpetual Apache war. Is that what you want? I need an answer, now."

Clem said, "I'll go along with your plan as long as it seems to be getting results. If we're led into an ambush, all bets are off. I hope you understand where I'm coming from."

"I understand," I told him. Secretly I hoped he could be constrained. I did not want to kill this grieving man, but I was convinced I would kill him if he let rage overcome his reason.

Nick continued to run his knife over leather. I could not read the varmint man's mind, but I hoped he too understood the big picture. As for killing him, I had grave doubts I could do that under any circumstances. Was this an indication of my affection for him? I just did not know at the time.

The moon was a sliver in the sky when we rode to the entrance of Superstition Mountain. Dahteste met us alone as she promised. Dismounted, she led us into the labyrinth of the sacred mountain to a place where we were safe from prying eyes and ears.

Seated in a circle on the ground, with our horses tied on a string line against a cliff, Dahteste said, "The braves you're looking for are eight in number. They are considered outlaws by our chief. If they can be killed in such a way that the authorities will know they're the cause of our latest spate of violence, we all can benefit."

"How are we going to do that?" Clem asked.

I raised my hand to silence him. "Clem, Dahteste and I will find a way to do this."

I needed now to reassure the Apache scout. "Dahteste, Clem Logan lost his wife and children in the raid. He witnessed the braves killing his family."

The Apache squaw said, "I understand such a loss. We will have justice together."

Nick drew his Bowie knife and ran its edge along a leather thong. "Do the eight braves live in your villages, or do they live alone?"

"They live alone. They are impetuous and brash. They are blinded by their feeling of self-worth. They are also superstitious."

I asked, "Dahteste, what's on your mind?"

"I can lead a company of cavalry to attack their camp."

"What about the three of us?"

"If you want to kill the leader and seize your cattle, you can ride with us. Together we will outgun the outlaws and prevail."

I asked her, "Where and when should we meet you?"

"Next Wednesday we leave the fort at daybreak. We'll be two miles south of here by early afternoon. Meet us where the trails come together. Be fully armed. When the shooting starts, kill only the Apaches in the small encampment. After the shooting, you'll identify the cattle that are yours. The cavalry officer in charge will let you take that herd once you sign the papers for them."

We stood and fetched our horses to retrace our path to the entrance of Superstition Mountain. At the entry, we heard the sounds of a lone horse passing through the desert. I thought I saw a pale white horse without a rider. That distraction gave Dahteste her chance to disappear.

I led Nick and Clem back to the ranches through the night. I left them at dawn with further instructions for our Wednesday meeting. I advised rest and caution while they prepared the pens at the Logan Ranch for the return of the remnants of Clem's herd.

We three rode to the rendezvous loaded with arms and ammunition. Each carried a rifle and wore bandoliers of ammunition. I carried two pistols, one on either hip. There could be no mistake we were a hunting party looking for well-armed men.

As Dahteste said, she came at the head of a cavalry company riding next to the captain and his guidon carrier. She raised her hand in greeting as the riders converged with us.

"Captain," I said, "we are hoping to accompany you to retrieve this man's herd of cattle, rustled by the Apache braves we're seeking. Is that all right with you?"

The captain touched the brim of his hat and said, "Feel free to suit yourself. We plan to charge the Apache position in an encircling movement and to kill them all. We'll need proof of ownership to surrender the cattle. Once you provide that, the herd is yours. Any questions?"

Nick asked, "On which side of your formation should we ride?"

The captain answered, "Ride on the right and back a few horses' lengths. The only rule is not to cross in front of my men. If you do, you're likely to be shot in error."

The captain ordered his men to form a line abreast. He ordered them forward at a trot, which turned into a canter and, finally, a gallop. Nick, Clem and I rode on the right side to the rear of the charge. Dahteste was riding in advance showing the way.

When the camp came into view, the cavalry trumpet sounded the charge. The horses were foaming at the mouth and straining as the soldiers began to shoot.

I saw only four Apache braves in the camp. Dahteste signaled toward the left. There I saw the missing four braves charging the soldiers from the left. I wheeled left and rode straight for those four. Clem and Nick rode in my wake. The cavalry kept charging ahead as if nothing was happening on their left flank.

It was clear to me that the approaching Apaches would easily have killed many soldiers in an undetected surprise action. I sighted down my rifle. At a gallop, I placed a bullet through the head of the brave who led the charge. Clem simultaneously shot the brave who was following the leader. Nick waited to fire until the two dead braves hit the ground. He threw down his rifle and, with his reins in his teeth, raised his two pistols and rode between the surviving two braves. He shot both braves, one on either side of him. They hit the ground and made the dust fly.

Meanwhile, the soldiers were checking that the four braves in the camp were dead. The sergeant and a private were checking on the rustled cattle, which were confined to a crowded pen.

Clem rode straight for the cattle pen to identify his herd. Nick rode back to pick up his rifle. I rode over to Dahteste.

"Dahteste, everything worked according to plan except for the flanking action of the four braves. How can we account for that?"

"The braves are Apaches. No leader would have left his camp vulnerable. Why do you think I advised the captain to place you in the rear and on the right?"

"I have to admit, that was the right call. You've done well. Thank you for your help."

I pointed toward the cattle pen where Clem was signing a piece of paper.

"It appears Clem has claimed his herd."

Nick rode up to thank Dahteste. "That was a good plan, well executed."

Dahteste said, "You'd better help your friend with his cattle."

As Clem and Nick got the herd moving, I sat on my mount beside Dahteste as the cavalry harvested the eight corpses and tied their lifeless bodies across their mounts.

The captain said, "Dahteste, we're ready to escort the dead to your chief. Please lead the way."

Dahteste nodded farewell to me. She rode forward, and the cavalry followed her at a walk as befitted a funeral cortege. I watched the slow procession guessing the chief would meet the procession and take charge of the bodies of his outlaw braves. At least, I hoped that would happen.

When they passed over the low horizon, I turned my horse to follow the trail of the herd and the two cowboys who were keeping them on track.

The ride home was more than a single day's ride, so Clem, Nick and I pitched camp. I made us chow over an open fire. We talked about the raid to recover the cattle as the sun went down.

"You were right, Carrie. I didn't trust your friend until the whole event was over. I thought for a moment she had alerted the braves to our coming."

"Clem, I wasn't sure what was happening on the left flank except we had to take action or lose more than a few good men."

Nick said, "We got lucky."

I laughed. "In every fight, the victors must get lucky. Are you complaining?"

"My only complaint is that I had to drop my best rifle in the sand so I could raise both my six-shooters."

"You'll clean your rifle good as new. As for your holding your reins in your mouth as you charged those braves, it was a picture. If I were an artist, I'd paint you riding right between those mustang mounts shooting both braves at the same time. Two head shots at a gallop isn't half bad."

Nick smiled. "I might be a little out of practice."

Clem shook his head. "If you were out of practice, I wonder how you would have fared in practice."

We had a little fun around that fire. While Clem checked his herd after sundown, Nick and I settled back on our saddles.

"I noticed your friend didn't do any shooting as the cavalry charged that camp."

"Do you resent that?"

"No. I just wanted to put the fact on the record."

"Dahteste is an Apache, and proud of it. The US cavalry did the dirty work the Apaches could not do on their own. When the bodies reach the chief, he will treat them in the Apache way. Meanwhile, the captain will take the proof that the eight Indians were rustlers to the fort. For a while, the Apache wars will have a truce—until the next outbreak of violence."

"There's one thing I don't understand."

"What's that, Nick?"

"When we got to the entry of Superstition Mountain, I thought I saw a pale white horse gallop past."

"I saw that horse too."

"When I looked around, Dahteste was gone."

"That's right."

"So, what really happened?"

"Nick, we were trespassing on sacred Indian land. Superstition Mountain is named for a reason. That horse has been running at midnight as long as the Apaches have been in the Territory. No one knows whether it's real or just a spirit. The Apaches worship it."

"We were taking a big chance going into the labyrinth with that Apache scout."

"She was taking the same risk."

"I don't think we were alone in there with her."

"Count on it that we weren't alone."

"So, who was in there with us?"

"Dahteste's powerful friend Lozen, a female Apache warrior just like her, only bigger and stronger, a better scout and tougher spirit. That's Dahteste's opinion, not mine."

"You knew this but didn't inform Clem, or me?"

"Lozen posed no danger to us except for the moment you honed your Bowie knife."

"What do you suppose she did during that interval?"

"I don't have to suppose—I know what she did. She drew her arrow back to her ear and waited. If you had threatened to use your weapon, she would have let that arrow fly straight through your right eye."

"Ouch!"

"Don't worry. You wouldn't have felt a thing."

Clem came back from checking his herd. He lay on his saddle and asked, "Who wouldn't have felt a thing?"

I said, "Don't worry. There's no harm done. Is your herd doing all right?"

"It's doing fine for now. I hope the coyotes don't get noisy in the night."

"Clem, the raid we did today was to set things right for you. How do you feel about what happened?"

"I'm of a mixed mind, Carrie. I saw justice done. I had a hand in that, for which I am grateful. I got back all but two of my cattle. But what I did—what we all did—won't bring Millie or the children back. They're gone for good."

I nodded. "That's what I concluded after Nick, and I killed the five murderers who slew my husband, Sam. Still, I did my duty. Sam appeared to me in a dream. He said he was satisfied. He told me to get on with my life. I hope Millie and the children will come into your dreams to say the same thing to you."

We did not talk much after that. I watched the shooting stars in the inky black sky until I fell asleep. At daybreak, the mooing of cattle brought me to my feet. I made coffee and passed out biscuits and jerky. We got to driving the herd while our shadows were still long on the desert floor.

We stayed one more night in the desert and another day droving before we reached the Logan Ranch. I bid goodbye to the two men and rode back to the Wells Ranch. I did a quick ride around my property. All was well despite my absence. I made a mental list of a hundred chores, the first of which was to take a bath and clean my clothes and weapons thoroughly.

I heated water and filled my bathtub nearly to the brim. I wore my clothes into the tub and stripped while bathing. That way, my clothes became as clean as I did. After that, I hung out my clothes and cleaned my weapons and oiled them lightly. I laughed to see myself naked in the mirror. I reckoned I had a few more years of youth to my credit. I also thought about Nick and wondered when he was going to drop by for that meal I had offered him.

No matter how men do the arithmetic of justice, another form of math must be done in Heaven. I had avenged my husband's death, and Clem had avenged his family's murder. Nick had warned me that Jake and his pals had friends, but I had discounted them. As things turned out, I should not have been optimistic. Perhaps I should have pursued a few of their most powerful friends to set an example.

Three weeks after we returned with Clem's herd, I found a note tacked to my barn door. It read:

Revenge is coming for Jake and Ike and Bill and Charlie and Johnny.

Beware!

Your time is nigh.

I took down the note and rode to show it to Nick.

"Those are the names of the five men we killed in downtown Gilbert."

"The writer of the note seems to have forgotten I was involved in the shootings."

"What do you think we should do?"

Nick thought about this for a long while before he responded.

"We have three choices. We can enlist the cavalry. We can inform the sheriff and his deputy so they can form a posse. We can contact your Apache friends and appeal for their protection."

"I notice you did not enumerate leaving the Territory as a possible course of action."

"Would you actually do that?"

"No, probably not. I was tempted to sell out and leave when they killed Sam. I decided instead to stick it out."

"That leaves us with the three options I just gave you."

"I'm going to take all three options and see what happens."

"All right, but I want you to know, I'll fight beside you when you have to fight."

When I showed Clem the note, he said the same thing. I felt grateful to both men, but I knew we needed reinforcements well before my enemies mounted their attack.

The next time I rode to town, I took the note to the sheriff's office and showed it to him and his deputy. The two men shook their heads.

"We can't do anything until a crime has been committed. You don't even know who wrote the note."

"You're right, Sheriff. Good day."

"Ma'am, I should warn you about something. Don't go taking the law into your own hands. That will make you as guilty as if you had been the criminal who wrote that note."

I was seething with rage, but I restrained myself from answering him. I had another idea.

"Sheriff, do you happen to know who Jake's powerful friends are?"

"Ma'am, even if I did know the answer to that question, I'd be reluctant to tell you. Some powers in this Territory you don't want to know anything about. You can't touch them, and they can make life miserable for you."

"I presume you mean the railroad combines and the big interests out East?"

"I'm just saying it's often better to leave well enough alone."

"That's well and good, but I've been threatened. There's no mistaking that fact."

"And unfortunately, words are not deeds, or we'd be able to do something to help you right now."

"You've answered my question without having to be inconvenienced."

I rode immediately to the Army fort to talk with the Colonel.

"Colonel, you're the military power in the Territory. Will you please read this note and tell me what I can do about it?"

He read the note more than once. When he looked up at me, his answer was reflected in his eyes.

"This is clearly a threat. Unfortunately, there's nothing in the note implying a Federal interest should be taken. Even if there were, what could I do about the matter?"

"What am I supposed to do?"

"You'll have to do what you can to defend yourself and your property. When things clarify, you can raise interest in the authorities, of which I am only one. How things develop will depend on many factors."

"Thank you for your time," I told the man. "One last question, do you know of any other threats like the one I've just received?"

"I'm personally knowledgeable about several such threats, all concentrated in the central part of the Territory."

"By that you mean, the area of most interest to the railroad interests?"

"That would be pure speculation without the kind of proof that could be hard to find."

I knew I was not going to get help from the military. I hoped the powerful interests behind the threatening note did not control the US government's actions in the Territory. My only remaining recourse was to consult with my Apache friend again.

I put out my signals and waited for Dahteste to make contact.

It took her three weeks to come to my house, but she came at midnight as before.

"I hope all has turned out well for you since our last meeting."

"Yes. I hope the same goes for you. I want to thank you for what you did for my friends and me."

"What I did was in the mutual interests of your people and mine. What do you require now?"

"I'm being threatened. I've received a hostile note. I don't know when I'll be attacked, but when that happens, my enemies intend to kill me and destroy my ranch."

"How can I help you?"

"I'm not at all sure at this point. If I see a way you can help, I'll signal."

"I can talk with Lozen about informal surveillance of your ranch."

"I don't know whether that would be a productive use of her time. The trouble is, the note may contain a false threat."

"I'll discuss the matter with her. You know how to reach me. If you need to be sheltered by my tribe, I can arrange that instantly."

"Thank you, Dahteste. Goodbye."

I had now exhausted the three avenues of help I had outlined with Nick. I visited him in his dwelling to report progress.

"I thought you might have trouble gaining anyone's attention."

"Since we last spoke, has any other alternative passed through your mind?"

"Do you know a newspaperman named Ben Dauber?"

"I know his name. He seems to show up to gather news whenever misfortune strikes."

"Did you know his mother, Maud Dauber, is friendly with the railroad interests?"

"No, I didn't. How reliable is your information about that?"

"It's totally reliable. I've also learned the son, and his mother are not in complete agreement about supporting those powerful interests."

"And your point is what?"

"It can't hurt to show Ben Dauber the threatening note and get his take on what it might mean."

"That's at least doing something active rather than simply waiting for thugs to show up to kill me and burn my buildings to the ground."

"Carrie, if you're afraid, just stay with me here. I'll give you privacy. You can go home again when you feel it's safe to do so."

"You're the second person to offer me sanctuary in the last four weeks. I'm grateful, but if I go into hiding, the people from the interests will think they have won the fight. I'd rather die defending my life and property than slink into a cowardly retirement."

"Suit yourself. My offer stands anytime you want to take advantage of it. My guns are always loaded. If you need help in a shootout, just holler."

The varmint man was nothing if not consistent. Like my friend Dahteste, Nick stood ready to help me anytime. With that possibility clearly in mind, I went to find Ben Dauber. I found him interviewing the sheriff in Gilbert.

"Mr. Dauber, my name is Carrie Wells. I'd like a minute of your time."

The newshound looked me in the eyes and hesitated. Then he said, "Carrie Wells, widow of Samuel Wells of the Wells Ranch south of town?"

"That's right."

"You and a man named Nick Nicholson shot down a man named Jake Evans and four of his friends in the center of town."

"You are well informed."

"I'm in the news business. Do you have time for a first-person interview? I'd like to do a story on how a woman and a stranger managed to kill five of the meanest gunfighters in the Territory."

"Mr. Dauber, I'll agree to your interview if you'll do something for me in return."

The young man stood to full height. "What would you like me to do?"

I handed him the threatening note and said, "Interpret this note for me right now."

Dauber looked closely at the note. He turned it to the light and held it between his eyes and the noonday sun.

"This note was written by someone wanting to get revenge for the deaths of the five men you and Mr. Nicholson shot dead."

"That much I know. What can you tell me about who likely had an interest in seeing my husband and me dead and my ranch, the Wells Ranch, put up for grabs."

Dauber took me by the arm and led me to the saloon. He ordered a bottle of whisky and two shot glasses from the bartender. He took the bottle and glasses to a table in the darkest area near the back. He set the bottle on the table and gestured for me to sit across from him.

"I've seen this kind of note before," he said.

"Tell me what it means."

"It means you've been identified as a problem by the railroad interest. Has anyone offered you money for your land?"

"Not in many years, no."

"Did anyone make an offer to your husband for your ranch."

"Not to my knowledge. Sam would never have sold. It's our future. Buying the land took every penny we had."

"Jake Evans and his people often did dirty favors for the railroad interest. When you killed them, you opened yourself for revenge on an almost unimaginable scale."

"Tell me something I could not guess for myself."

"I know the proposed route of the rail spur between Phoenix and Tucson."

"That might be helpful if the rights of way extended through my land."

"I'll determine that, but I'll have to be careful. If the interest discovers I'm on their trail, I won't be able to see you again because I'll be dead."

"Oh, dear! I wouldn't want your blood on my hands."

"I can get closer to the truth than most people."

"Because your mother's Maud Dauber?"

"That's part of it, yes."

Dauber filled the two glasses and pushed one toward me. I don't usually drink liquor, but he was insistent.

"Drink with me. We'll have to make it look as if we spent the whole afternoon talking about the shooting. You've got plenty to tell me, I think, since you were also involved in the cavalry action against the Apache rustlers."

I nodded. Ben Dauber would eagerly listen to my accounts of the two shootings. In return, he would provide what I needed to know about the railroad interest. As we warmed to our discussions, we drank the whole bottle of whiskey.

A tough looking gunman came through the swinging doors of the saloon. He did not seem to be interested in drinking. Instead, he walked back looking for Ben Dauber and me.

"Mr. Dauber," he said, "my name is Silas Gorge. I work for Mr. Mason of the railroad."

"Mr. Gorge, as you can see, I'm entertaining this lady at present. Will you please wait until our interview is over?"

Gorge scowled and drew his gun. He shoved it in Dauber's face and cocked the trigger. I acted instinctively when I pulled my gun and shot the man through the right temple. He collapsed in a heap on the floor.

Dauber knelt to feel for the man's pulse. There was none. Dauber went to the bar and asked the saloonkeeper to fetch the sheriff. He took my pistol and shoved it in his belt. Then he escorted me to the second floor to an open room.

"Carrie, stay in this room. Don't come out until I call for you."

Ben Dauber went back downstairs. I could not hear what the men were saying, but the sheriff went to fetch his deputy. Together they lifted the corpse and carried it out of the saloon. Dauber came to the room where I was waiting.

"I know a back way out of this saloon. Come with me."

We went down the back stairway. He escorted me to my horse and handed over my gun.

"Do you have a place you can stay away from your ranch for two days?"

"Yes. What's going to happen?"

"I shot Silas Gorge, not you. Can you remember that?"

"But that's not true. I shot him because he was going to shoot you."

"Do you want to hang from the neck until you are dead?"

"No."

"I was threatened by a man who had the drop on me and would have killed me. I managed to shoot him because it was dark and he did not see I had a gun below the table."

"So, you shot him in self-defense."

"That's right. Now go to your secret dwelling. Where should I look for you in two days?"

"Go to the Logan Ranch. That's the one adjacent to the Wells Ranch, which is mine. Tell Clem Logan you need to see me. He'll lead you to me if you're alone."

"Fine. When you get where you're going, clean your six-shooter thoroughly. If anyone wants to know the last time it was fired, tell them you did target practice on your ranch. Have you got all that?"

"Yes. I'll be going now."

"Good. Under no circumstances are you to return to your own ranch until I give you the all clear."

"Thank you, Mr. Dauber."

"No, thank you, Mrs. Wells. You've given me some terrific stories. From the way you operate, we're going to have a great literary relationship—if you can stay alive."

I rode out of town, careful not to look like a fugitive. I went directly to Nick's place and told him I needed shelter for two days. He let me clean my weapon in his water barrel. As an afterthought, I told him mischief was going to be done to the Wells Ranch during the next forty-eight hours.

Nick picked up his weapons and talked with Clem for over an hour before the two of them set out toward the Wells Ranch.

I oiled my gun after I cleaned it. When it was reloaded, I shoved it under the cob pillow in the bed Nick had offered me. I waited in anguish thinking of what might be happening to my friends.

In the middle of the second night, I was awakened by the sounds of Nick getting ready for bed.

"I'm sorry if I woke you up, Carrie."

"What's been happening, Nick?"

"Don't you want to wait until morning to hear the story?"

I was fully awake. "If you're capable of telling me now, please do so."

"You surely do know how to throw a party. There must have been thirty men against Clem and me just after sundown. They came from every direction. We kept changing our firing positions within your house, but we had taken plenty of ammunition. By the third hour, we reckoned we had killed a dozen men. Then we heard a low rumbling sound like a herd of horses on the run. The shooting of the attackers was no longer directed at the house. We were being rescued, only the rescuers were not using rifles or hand guns."

"I'll bet the Apaches helped you."

"Yes. And there must have been two or three dozen braves. We stopped shooting and watched the action as best we could see it in the pitch black of night. Screams indicated the Apaches had used the tactic of wounding a few to instill fear in the others. Finally, all screams stopped. Dahteste and another fierce woman warrior came to the door to say it was over and the braves were taking scalps."

"Did Dahteste say anything else?"

"She asked if you were safe. I told her you were all right. She said to tell you that all debts were canceled now. She wished you well."

"Is that the whole story?"

"One more point, and then we'll have to get some sleep. Dahteste said not to worry about the dead. They would be taken care of."

I had no idea what Dahteste meant by that. Nick fell fast asleep. I knew he had told me everything he knew. I went to sleep as well.

The next morning everything was quiet until the sun had risen halfway to its summit. A knock on Nick's door revealed Ben Dauber and Clem.

Clem said, "This man says he knows you, Carrie."

"It's okay, Clem. Come in, Mr. Dauber. Watch your head as we have a low ceiling."

Nick was stirring, so I introduced him.

"Mr. Ben Dauber, newspaperman, this is Nick Nicholson, the varmint man. I think you'll have a lot to say to each other. Before that begins, I'll put on a pot of coffee and cut a loaf of bread. What news do you have for me, Mr. Dauber?"

The newshound looked at Nick, Clem and me as if we were alien creatures. I figured he was assessing how many stories he could write after interviewing us three.

He said, "First, Carrie, the railroad interests have decided on one big push to take your ranch once and for all."

"Ben," I said with a smile, "I think your news has been overtaken by events."

"What?" Ben said as I poured him a cup of hot coffee.

"Nick and Clem, why don't you tell him what's happened."

Nick smiled, and Clem gestured for him to speak to the reporter.

"Do you have the time for the whole story, Mr. Dauber, or do you want the short version?"

"Why don't you tell me the short version to whet my whistle first."

"There was a pale white horse, and its thundering hooves were heard in the desert when wrongs needed to be made right again. On this horse rode a ghost rider."

"I've heard that story before," Ben said.

"Well, it's true. Clem and I heard the horse's hooves and saw the ghost rider last night at the Wells Ranch. There was a terrific fight that lasted half the night, followed by silence. If we take the time after breakfast to ride over there, you'll see the result of the tumult."

We ate our breakfast in a rush. Then we saddled our horses and rode to the Wells Ranch. The place seemed deserted except the house was riddled with a thousand bullet holes, and sunlight streamed through them like golden rods. On the grounds were myriad horseshoe prints, but no bodies.

"See, Mr. Dauber, the ghost rider has come and gone. You can tell he's been here because of the bullet holes. I'd venture to say any threat to Carrie Wells' life or farm has been rendered null and void."

Ben Dauber pushed his hat back on his head. He addressed me directly.

"Mrs. Wells, may I use your dining room to interview Mr. Nicholson and Mr. Logan?"

"You may if you'll all stay for a picnic lunch. I'll make bean and bacon stew."

"That sounds perfect. Who will be my first interviewee?"

I said, "You have my story, Ben. Why don't you begin with Clem? Once he's done, it will be time for lunch. Then Nick can give you his stories."

I kept quiet as Ben did his interviews. He had lots of probing questions, but the men stood by their stories.

Around halfway through the afternoon, the sheriff and deputy dropped by. I fed them lunch while they did their business, which was an investigation into rumors they had heard from unnamed sources.

"We didn't expect you to be here, Mr. Dauber," said the sheriff.

"And we didn't expect you to be here either, Mrs. Wells," said the deputy. But the sheriff 'accidentally' stuck his elbow into Billy the Lawman's gut.

"What Billy means to say is we're delighted to have Mrs. Wells present since she's clearly safe from harm, contrary to rumors we heard in town."

Ben Dauber leaned forward as he motioned for me to serve the lawmen more of the delicious stew.

"Sheriff, you were saying Carrie Wells is safe from harm? What, pray, would have threatened her?"

"She brought a threatening note to our office, don't you know?"

"And you thought the threat had followed through?"

"Here's the living proof that what we heard was nonsense."

The sheriff and his deputy dug into their bowls of stew with gusto. I poured them glasses of water and put out the bread for them to eat.

The lawmen tired of Dauber's incessant questions. Finally, they departed without uttering a word about the way the house was admitting shafts of sunlight.

Ben Dauber sat back in his chair laughing at the discomfiture of the authorities.

"I don't suppose I'll ever learn the truth about what happened here last night."

"That makes four of us," Nick stated brightly.

"Well, I'll be heading out. It's getting dark, and I love riding in the night at this time of year."

"Keep an eye out for the ghost rider, Mr. Dauber," Clem told him.

Dauber smiled as he was a good sport.

"Any time you want another interview, you know where to find me," said Nick.

The newspaperman rode toward Gilbert with the sun tilting over the horizon. His shadow was a long, purple finger pointing East.

Clem was the next to depart. I bade him goodnight, sure he would get a sound night's sleep after whatever he had done the night before. He headed south toward his ranch.

Nick rose from his chair, but I had an impulse and pushed him down gently to stay.

"Nick Nicholson, varmint man, you let me sleep on your floor two nights running. Now you're going to sleep in my bed for a change, only I'm going to be in there with you. What do you say to that?"

"I say it's high time we got better acquainted, Carrie. Do you mind if I wash my weapons before we hit the hay?"

I wanted to say, "Glory, Hallelujah!" Instead, I said, "I'll heat the water. Put your clothes on the chair and climb into the tub. It's a proper bath you'll be having, and you're going to share it with me."

Contributors

Joanna Blair

Joanna has an extensive background working in theatre and dance. She's written for Splickety and Keys for Kids as well as three plays which have been produced in the US and Malta.

Steve Carr

Steve lives in Richmond, Virginia and began his writing career as a military journalist. He has had over 170 short stories published internationally in print and online magazines, literary journals and anthologies.

Sand, a collection of his short stories, was published recently by Clarendon House Books. His plays have been produced in several states in the U.S.

Steve was a 2017 Pushcart Prize nominee.

You can connect with him on Facebook at: Facebookhttps://www.facebook.com/profile.php?id= 100012966314127

On Twitter via: @carrsteven960.

E. W. Farnsworth

E. W. is a master of the nineteenth-century western story. His collections of stories about the Old West in the Arizona Territories are a classic of the genre.

Many of his tales first appeared in Zimbell House anthologies.

Matthew Gowans

Matthew is a short story and fiction writer living in Prestwick, Scotland.

He is currently experimenting with several genres, including sci-fi, horror, and Western.

Andrea Hargrove

Andrea is very happy to write about trails because that's where she gets some of her best ideas. Her usual trails to hike are the Appalachian Trail and a few local trails near her home in Pennsylvania, but she tries to get some variety in her travels both physical and literary.

This is Andrea's second published work. Her first short story, *The Fairy Maze*, can be found in the Zimbell House anthology *A Nymph's Tale*.

She loves to hear from her readers, who can contact her via Twitter @AndreaJHargrove.

Ingrid Alice Lohr

Ingrid lives in Central New York among the farmlands with her collection of pets.

She has loved the craft of storytelling since she was able to speak.

Jerome McFadden

Jerome's stories have appeared in previous Zimbell House anthologies, including *The Neighbors,* and *River Tales.*

His stories have also been read on stage by the Liar's League in Hong. One of his stories was also nominated as one of the best crime stories on the web.

He now lives and writes out of eastern Pennsylvania.

Leslie D. Soule

Leslie received her M.A. in English from National University. She is a scholar, artist, citizen journalist, and martial artist. She has been an established writer for a decade.

What sets her work apart from the pack, is its intensity in dealing with the ultimately personal journey of life and its myriad setbacks and sorrows. Her novels contain a deeply populist, anti-establishment tone, one in which rebellion against the often-authoritarian norm is praised. Her work embraces the outcasts of society–the discarded, the rebels, the people that the magazines forgot to tell you, exist.

Readers enjoy Soule's no-nonsense, fast-paced style of writing. She loves to hear from her readers, and encourages them to connect with her on Twitter, and to help spread the word, about her work. Twitter: @Falcondraco

Other Anthologies from Zimbell House

The Mysteries of Suspense
Romantic Morsels
The Steam Chronicles
Pagan
Tales from the Grave
The Adventures of Pirates
Curse of the Tomb Seekers
Travelers
Dark Monsters
On a Dark and Snowy Night
Where Cowboys Roam
The Key
Veil of Secrets
Tournament Games
The Lost Door
Nocturnal Natures
It's an Urban Style of Love
The Neighbors
Date Night
Why? A Collection of Mysterious Tales
The Mountain Pass
River Tales
After Effect
Morsels from the Chef
Ghost Stories
Second Chance
Children of Zeus Attack of the Federation
A Nymph's Tale
Hades Had a Son
If I Say No
Poseidon's Daughter
No Trace

Coming Soon from Zimbell House

I'm *Dead?*

The Way of Artemis

Midnight Rising

Aphrodite's Curse

Not Anyone's Wife

Shifting

Join our mailing list to receive updates on new releases, discounts, bonus content, and other great books from

Or visit us online to sign up:

http://www.ZimbellHousePublishing.com

A Note from the Publisher

How to Thank a Contributor

Dear Reader,

Everyone at Zimbell House Publishing would like to thank you for reading *Trail's End*. If you would like to thank a particular contributor, the best way is to leave a review for them. You may do so by leaving one on our Goodreads page, under the *Trail's End* title, by using the link below and be sure to mention the contributor directly:

http://www.goodreads.com/ZimbellHousePublishing

Why should you leave a review? Reviews help budding authors build their credibility in the book industry. By posting a review on Goodreads or other sites, you help other readers find new authors they may wish to follow, and you never know, your review may end up on an author's website one day.

Friend us on Goodreads:
https://www.goodreads.com/ZimbellHousePublishing

Follow us on Facebook:
https://www.facebook.com/ZimbellHousePublishing/

Follow us on Twitter:
http://twitter.com/ZimbellHousePub